The Last Train to Paris

A Novel

Hamon de Quillan

Global East-West. London

Contents

1
Boarding the Storm

The train jolted suddenly, throwing Emma against the cold, leather seat. Outside the window, the sky darkened rapidly, thick clouds swallowing the horizon as the storm grew fierce. Every thunderclap rattled her bones, echoing the chaos within her. She clutched her bag tightly, as if anchoring herself to a world unraveling. Her breath hitched, her heart pounding a frantic rhythm like the storm pounding the roof above her. The scent of rain and fear hung heavy in the air, and she felt the weight of everything she'd lost pressing down, suffocating her.

She had fled London in the late afternoon, leaving behind a shattered life. Words like betrayal, disillusionment, and loss replayed in her mind. Her engagement was broken, not gently, but with the cruel finality of a shattered mirror. The gallery where she had poured her soul was no longer her sanctuary but a cold, empty shell of betrayal—the embezzlement that had come to light was just the surface. Her career lay in ruins, her dreams scattered like broken glass, and all she had left was a single letter from her grandmother, whispering of a secret treasure hidden in a Montmartre apartment. The irony of clutching a map to her past amid the storm's rage was not lost on her. She felt like a leaf caught in a whirl, tossed from one wave of despair to another.

Across the aisle, Liam sat rigid, his face pale beneath the shadows cast by storm-lit flicker. Normally, he'd be scribbling in his notebook, chasing a story, but tonight, his pen was still. His thoughts circled the chaos in his mind—like Emma, he was fleeing something, though his was quiet. The weight of unspoken fears pressed against his chest, the gnawing reminder that he might never find the inspiration he sought. The storm roared louder, towering like a judgment against their fragile worlds. He kept glancing at her, noticing the tense set of her shoulders, the faint tremor in her hands as she clutched her bag like a talisman. In her eyes, he glimpsed a storm far darker than the one outside—a turmoil that haunted her, a secret she dare not reveal. A flicker of curiosity ignited within him; beneath her composed exterior lay a story waiting in the shadows.

Suddenly, the train lurched again, a sickening sway that knocked Emma's sketchbook from her lap. She hurriedly grabbed it, her fingers trembling as she flipped through pages filled with intricate drawings—not casual doodles but detailed plans of the train's layout, security routes, and hidden alcoves. Liam watched her with rising suspicion, an ache of instinct telling him she was more than she appeared. When he finally touched her arm, she jerked back, eyes wide with nerves.

"Why are you drawing all this?" he asked softly, voice edged with cautious curiosity.

Emma hesitated, biting her lip, then looked away, her face a mask of calm—an act, surely.

"It's nothing," she whispered. "Just something to keep my mind busy."

Liam's journalist mind accused her of hiding something, yet her trembling voice betrayed her. The silence between them grew heavier, thick with secrets neither wanted to confess.

Later that night, the storm's fury intensified as the train came to a sudden halt in Amiens. Light flickered ominously through fractured windows, casting ghostly shadows into the carriage. Emma, restless and unable to sleep, caught Liam speaking softly into his phone, his voice hurried and cautious—like he was hiding something. She couldn't understand every word, but snippets reached her ears—the package, deadline, the next move. Her breath caught, a stone settling cold in her stomach. Her grandmother's letter suddenly felt alive with ominous meaning, whispering warnings in the dark. What if this wasn't just a storm delay? What if they had walked headfirst into something dangerous—something more delicate and deadly than she'd imagined? Her trembling hands clenched her sketchbook tighter, her mind racing with possibilities that chilled her blood, each new revelation tightening the noose of her hidden past.

Throughout the night, Emma's thoughts spun like a web—twisting memories, fears, and questions into a tangled knot. She kept recalling her grandmother's words about a "treasure," but not the kind buried in gold or jewels. It was something far more elusive—evidence, perhaps, of a betrayal that stretched decades behind her, tangled in the dust of history. Her prior life as an investigator resurfaced with painful clarity; she had once hunted con artists and forgeries, unraveling lies hidden beneath paintings and photographs. That same instinct now told her she was walking into a trap, a story far more dangerous than a simple theft. Liam's presence beside her was unpredictable—an ally, or perhaps a threat. She could see it now—there were layers she hadn't yet peeled away, secrets buried beneath the storm outside, waiting for the dawn to reveal them all, casting long shadows over their fragile alliance.

***

The train lurched unexpectedly as the storm outside churned the sky into a mess of dark clouds. Liam sat by the window, staring at the blurred landscape, feeling like the world was tipping out of focus. His pen rested uselessly in his hand, his mind unable to settle on anything concrete, as if the chaos swirling outside mirrored the turmoil within. The delay stretched into hours, and with each passing minute, he felt that urgency growing—an itch that refused to be scratched, a story that refused to reveal itself. He had come seeking clarity, a spark to ignite his words again, but what he found instead was a thick silence, broken only by distant thunder and the soft rustling of Emma's sketch-book beside him.

As the train shuddered to a halt in a dimly lit station, Liam glanced over at Emma. She had closed her sketchpad, her brow furrowed, eyes distant. There was something in the way she carried herself—a quiet tension that didn't fit her calm veneer. He wondered what secrets she kept hidden beneath her composed exterior. Minutes later, they found themselves sharing a cramped compartment, forced into proximity by circumstance. At first, their conversations were cautious, guarded by the unspoken understanding that trust might be a luxury they couldn't afford. But with the storm pounding on the metal walls and the night deepening outside, barriers began to break down. Liam asked about her art, and Emma hesitated before revealing she was a restorer, shyly explaining her fascination with details and hidden stories woven into cracked canvases and old murals. Liam, hungry for distraction, talked about his travels through Europe, describing train routes and forgotten towns—stories that seemed to float from his lips like relics, waiting to be rediscovered.

Then came the first twist, almost quietly slipping

into their dialogue like a shadow. Liam's gaze sharpened when he noticed Emma's notebook. Her sketches weren't random doodles—they were detailed architectural diagrams of the train car itself. Lines and symbols marked every emergency exit, staff station, camera lens, and hidden corner. His heart quickened. He leaned in slightly, unsure whether to confront or simply observe. Emma caught him looking and snapped the book shut, cheeks flushing. She mumbled something about calming nerves, but Liam couldn't shake the feeling that her drawings held secrets—something beyond her quiet reassurance. The train's rhythmic clatter masked their whispers, but the weight of unspoken questions hung thick in the air.

Later that night, as the train lingered in Amiens, Liam's phone buzzed with eerie silence. Emma, curled against her seat, watched him as he fidgeted, then excused himself for a moment. When he returned, his face tight, he seemed different—more guarded. Emma caught a glimpse of his phone, and her stomach clenched. He had been speaking in hurried, hushed Arabic—a language he had never mentioned before—about "the package" and "tomorrow's deadline." Her heartbeat quickened as the familiar flicker of suspicion ignited. The letter from her grandmother, once seen as a simple fragment of family history, now loomed larger. What if she was walking into something dangerous? Had her quest for the truth led her onto a route paved with secrets darker than she had imagined? The storm outside raged harder, as if echoing the rising tension in her chest.

The deeper Liam and Emma delved, the more their worlds revealed themselves to be entwined in uncovered layers of deception. Emma's past as an insurance investigator specializing in art fraud surfaced suddenly, a piece she had kept hidden under layers of artistic calm. Her real mission wasn't just to find a treasure but to uncover evidence of a vast forgery ring shadowing history—stolen art traded under the guise of sale, hidden in plain sight. The letter from her grandmother wasn't just a cryptic message but a hint toward critical documents buried beneath Montmartre, relics that could blow open the entire operation. Meanwhile, Liam's cover story—travel writer—masking a covert role with Interpol—began to make sense. His crusade against smuggling and art theft intertwined with Emma's search, both driven by a web of criminal factions growing more nervous and desperate.

The realization hit like a turning tide. They had both become targets—not random victims but carefully selected pieces in a larger game. Their delayed train, the storm's fury, the suspicious passengers—all orchestrated. Their allies, friends smiling kindly in the dim glow of the compartment, the helpful conductor with his well-timed coffees—all woven into the web of deception. The moment came quietly, almost stealthily—a final tease—when they discovered their phones had been cloned, all messages erased or rerouted. Emma's heart hammered. Her grandmother's hiding place in Montmartre wasn't just a refuge; it was a fortress, a labyrinth built by Resistance members long ago, filled with secret passages and hidden chambers. Emma could feel the weight of history pressing down—each shadow in that old city concealing stories of betrayal, heroism, and silent complicity. The walls of her own family's legacy seemed to crumble at her feet as she stared at the crumbling bricks, wondering if revelations were just waiting behind every cracked stone.

And then came the betrayal—shocking and immediate. Liam's voice on the line with his handler revealed the terrible truth: Emma's investigation had been compromised from the very start. Someone within her own circle had betrayed her, feeding information to those she hunted. The sting of that thought sliced deep, but what cut even deeper was the revelation that her grandmother, Margot, who she believed had died decades ago, was alive—and the mastermind behind it all. She had been orchestrating the entire operation, hiding her true nature behind layers of deception. Emma's mind raced, her heartbeat pounding in her ears. The woman who had once been her hero, her protector, was now the face of their greatest enemy. Every step she took had led her into a trap, and the shadows of Montmartre now seemed more threatening than ever—little did they know, the storm still howled, and Emma and Liam's fight was only just beginning.

***

The sky grew darker with each passing hour as the train ground to a halt amidst a furious winter storm. The wind howled like a beast outside, rattling the windows and stirring unease in every passenger's chest. Emma sat stiffly in her seat, clutching her bag as if it could anchor her to some semblance of calm. Her eyes flicked to the dimly lit corridor, every shadow stretching unnaturally, whispering secrets she couldn't quite hear. She felt the weight of her unspoken fears pressing down, as if the storm itself might swallow them whole before dawn. No one knew how long they'd be stranded, and that silence—thick, suffocating—became an uninvited guest that lingered in the cramped carriage.

Outside, the rain pounded relentlessly, turning the world outside into a swirling mess of gray. The pounding echoed through the train's bones, drowning out the faint hum of conversation and the occasional cough. Emma's mind drifted to the letter her grandmother had left her—cryptic instructions, a promise of something hidden in Montmartre—something that suddenly seemed even further away in this chaos. She thought of how she'd escaped London's betrayal, fleeing her shattered life with trembling hope. Now, instead of smooth tracks and distant horizons, she faced an unpredictable storm that could trap her here forever. Every minute stretched longer, as if time itself had decided to pause, to watch her withholding breath. The wind whispered outside, sounding like a warning she couldn't hear.

Liam gaze was fixed on the dark window, chewing his lower lip as he listened to the storm's fury. His journalistic instincts fought against the rising anxiety; he had come here seeking stories, not more silence. The train's usual rhythm was broken, replaced by an eerie stillness that felt unnatural, almost sinister. Normally, the train's hum would be a comforting drone, but tonight, it felt like a prelude to something worse. His fingers tapped nervously on his notebook, searching for words that wouldn't come. His mind wandered to images of conflict, chaos—places where the storm outside paled in comparison to the storms within. Something was off. The delayed departure, the sudden halt—these weren't ordinary weather issues. They were signs, signals he couldn't yet decipher but sensed deep in his bones.

Across from him, Emma pulled out her sketchbook and began to draw with swift, confident strokes. Her hand moved almost automatically, capturing the contours of the emergency hatch, the security cameras, the faint outlines of staff stations—all details she'd memorized during her brief stint working undercover. She knew these sketches weren't just art; they were a map, a covert record of the train's layout, its vulnerabilities. She had learned long ago to keep her fears silent, burying them beneath her sketches. Drawing calmed her, a mental anchor in the swirling darkness. Yet tonight, her eyes flicked up every so often, watching Liam. She wondered if he'd noticed her unusual note-taking, or if her secret was safe, buried beneath the lines of graphite. Still, she couldn't shake the feeling that she was no longer alone in her quiet vigilance.

Later that night, the train lurched unexpectedly as another gust of wind battered the carriage. Liam's phone vibrated, but he kept his gaze fixed outside as if he could will the storm to pass. When he finally retrieved it, a brief glance revealed a message in Arabic, hurriedly typed. Emma, seated nearby, saw his brow furrow as he typed back, voice tense and hurried. He claimed he was ordering room service, but she caught the faint, hurried inflection in his voice, the hurried exchange he tried to conceal. Her heart kicked up a beat as she listened, noting the words he kept repeating: "the package," "tomorrow's deadline," whispered like a secret in the dark. Her grandmother's letter flickered again in her mind, suddenly feeling heavier with unspoken truths. What if her journey—and Liam's—wasn't just about art, or lost treasures, but something far more dangerous? As the storm raged outside, suspicion crept into her thoughts, threading into her bones.

Emma's stomach clenched as she watched Liam's restless movements. She remembered her past—her days hunting for signs of forged art, her nights dodging those who sought to silence her. Was she destined to stumble blindly into a web spun long before she arrived? The sketchpad, the whispered phone calls, the strange signals—they all added up, a puzzle she was only beginning to understand. The train, once a vessel of fleeting escape, now felt like a trap, and she wondered who was truly behind the storm. Was it nature, or something darker? That question gnawed at her, raising hairs on her neck. Her hand trembled slightly as she closed her sketchbook, the weight of her secret pressing against her chest. Somewhere beyond the storm, danger loomed—silent, lurking—ready to strike when least expected.

2
Stranded in Chaos

The train had been stranded in the dark for hours now, a heavy silence pressing down like an unseen weight. Emma's eyes flicked around the carriage, half-expecting something to break the quiet, but only shadows moved in the flickering overhead lights. She sat curled in her seat, her sketchpad forgotten on her lap, her fingers trembling slightly. Every sound seemed amplified—the distant rumble of the storm outside, the faint shuffle of passengers trying to find comfort, the quiet hum of the engine that refused to turn on again. In the dim glow of her newfound solitude, Emma felt the strange pull of the shadows that danced along the walls, like unspoken secrets lurking just beyond reach.

Liam, sitting across the aisle, sensed an unspoken tension in the air. His gaze lingered on Emma, noticing how her jaw was clenched, her eyes fixed on some distant point. They had exchanged few words since the train stopped; he'd felt the thick wall of her silence, a kind of barricade she had thrown up. His own nerves were tense, a familiar ache in his chest reminding him that no amount of journalistic curiosity could drown the feeling of impending danger. The storm outside raged beyond the windows, streaks of lightning illuminating the curtains fluttering in the draft. Every flash revealed brief glimpses of their faces—a snapshot of hesitation and uncertainty—before plunging them back into darkness.

As minutes stretched into what felt like hours, Emma noticed something strange. Her eyes caught Liam's brief glance toward her, then away, as if he was trying not to look. Without realizing it, her gaze shifted to his hands, which rested tightly on his notebook. She spotted the faint creases of concentration on his brow, an almost palpable tension that matched her own. She wondered what secrets he carried behind his calm exterior. Somewhere in that quiet, shadowed space, beneath the layers of their own worries, an unspoken understanding began to form—neither of them was alone in this darkness. Shadows stretched between them, not just in the dim light, but in the silent exchange of wary glances and cautious breaths.

Suddenly, a faint metallic clang echoed from the corridor, jerking both of them from their thoughts. Emma's heart skipped a beat. Years of training bit into her mind, telling her to stay calm, to observe.

Liam's eyes sharpened, and he subtly edged forward, inching toward the door. Outside, shadows flickered just beyond the frosted glass, shifting as if alive. She clutched her sketchpad tighter, feeling her stomach tighten with a strange mixture of fear and curiosity. The storm's howling outside seemed to fade, replaced by an almost unnatural silence that made every breath sound louder. This was no ordinary storm; it was a disruption, a catalyst for what was to come. Shadows were no longer just darkness; they were the silence waiting to be broken.

In that haunting quiet, Liam moved closer to her, his voice barely above a whisper.

" We need to stay alert," he murmured, eyes scanning the corridor, sensing that every shadow might hide more than darkness.

Emma nodded slowly, her mind racing with questions. What was that sound? Could it have been a break-in? Or was it simply the train settling after hours of chaos? Still, the feeling persisted—there was something wrong beneath the surface of this frozen night, something they both felt but couldn't quite name. Shadows grew darker, and the silence stretched on, thick with anticipation. Somehow, in this stillness, they both knew that the real confrontation had yet to begin—hidden in shadows, waiting patiently for its moment to reveal itself.

***

The dim glow of the reading lamp cast long shadows across the cramped compartment. Emma leaned against the window, gazing at the blurred landscape outside, each passing town a fleeting memory. Her sketchbook rested on her thighs, open to a page filled with hurried lines and detailed notes, not just doodles but plans—plans that felt like wild seeds planted in uncertain soil. She had become an expert at hiding her true self behind calm eyes, but watching Liam fumble with his phone, she sensed something beneath his composed expression. The quiet hum of the engine and the distant crackle of static from the radio were their only company, a reminder that in this moving metal cocoon, they were trapped, caught between past and uncertain future.

Liam looked up from his device, stealing a glance at Emma, who appeared lost in thought. Despite the storm swirling outside and the chaos that had brought them together, he felt an inexplicable pull. Their circumstances had forced them into this tiny space, yet in that closeness, something sincere was budding—an ember of connection in a time of shared danger. He had never believed in the power of stories, but here he was, capturing more than words—capturing the unspoken, the subtle tremors of nerves and hope flickering in her eyes. His own heart pounded with a strange mixture of anticipation and exhaustion, the kind that comes from walking the edge of the unknown.

Suddenly, Liam's attention was drawn to Emma's sketches once more, noticing the precise lines, the careful shading that hinted at more than artistic talent. His professional curiosity tingled—these weren't mere sketches born out of boredom or nerves. They were architectural, deliberate, noting security cameras, emergency exits, and even the positions of the train staff. Emma quickly shut the book, cheeks flushing, as if caught in a lie. But her fingers trembled slightly, betraying her. Liam's mind raced—was there something she wasn't telling him? The flickering candle of trust seemed fragile now, yet undeniable, sparking questions that refused to fade. In the tense silence, they both understood that truths, once revealed, could change everything.

The train slowed abruptly, lurching in the night. Outside, the storm unleashed its fury, thunder trembling like distant artillery. A voice crackled over the intercom, announcing a delay, then another, each message more uncertain than the last. The lights flickered, and the atmosphere thickened with unease. Emma's breath caught amid the chaos—they were no longer just stranded; they were caught in a trap with no clear way out. Shadows danced in the corners of the compartment, and Emma felt her pulse quicken. Something was off—beyond the storm, beyond the weather. Strangers, friends, even familiar faces, suddenly felt like dangers concealed beneath polite smiles. A ripple of dread spread through her, an instinct whispering to be alert.

Later that night, in the sparse and flickering corridor light, Emma saw Liam's phone glow in the dark. She hesitated, then edged closer, catching the faint echo of his voice through the screen. He was speaking in a language she didn't understand, rapid, tense. The words slipped out—package, deadline, tomorrow. Her heart pounded as her thoughts flashed to her grandmother's letter, its mention of hidden treasure, and secret rooms filled with history. Could there be a connection? Was Liam part of something she hadn't yet guessed? The pieces banged together like a puzzle she had yet to see clearly, filling her with a cautious mix of dread and curiosity. In that cramped space, the weight of secrets pressed down hard, and neither of them could pretend anymore that this was just about a delayed train.

As dawn approached, the atmosphere in their carriage shifted—colder, more dangerous. Emma's mind raced with revelations. She was not just an art restorer; her past was steeped in investigations—disguises, false identities, undercover missions. The treasure her grandmother's letter hinted at was more than a box of paintings; it was a bundle of evidence, long hidden, that could expose a vast art forgery network rooted in WWII. Her motives were personal, driven by a need for closure and justice. She had thought her search was about her grandmother's memory, but now it seemed tied to her very identity—her purpose intertwined with uncovering decades of deception.

Meanwhile, Liam's true background emerged from the shadows. His travel writer cover was nothing but a mask for an undercover role in Interpol's fight against smuggling. The train routes, the delays—they were not mere accidents. They were part of a careful plan to contain a network still operating from the ruins of history. His panic attacks, which once seemed unexplainable, now made sense—they weren't just stress; they were the aftermath of living a double life on the edge of danger, where every corner could hide an assassin or a snare. Together, in the confined space of metal and storm, they started to see that their missions overlapped like threads woven into one unbreakable fabric—a fabric their enemies sought to cut apart.

The realization dawned sharply: they weren't just random strangers pressed against circumstance—they were targets. Their suspect passengers, their smiling conductors, even the helpful stranger with the coffee—all could be part of the shadowy crime network. Emma's gut clenched as she remembered the subtle hints— an overheard whisper, a suspicious glance, the way Liam's phone vibrated as if watched. Their communication was compromised, their plans monitored. Every message, every step they took, was shadowed by unseen eyes. The truth hit hard—this storm was merely a curtain hiding the real tempest. Out in the dark, danger lurked, silent and deadly, waiting for them to let their guard down. All the while, Emma's mind raced, contemplating that the hidden apartment in Montmartre, the secret passages, might hold the keys to everything. But reaching it meant risking everything, standing face-to-face with the past she thought she understood—and with the woman who had engineered it all, her grandmother.

***

The train shuddered to a halt, and in the dim, flickering light of the carriage, Emma felt her pulse quicken. It was late, and the sudden stop had turned the space into a cocoon of silence, broken only by the muted hum of the engine cooling beneath them. She sat by the window, her sketchbook resting on her lap, but her gaze was fixed elsewhere—on the man across from her. Liam was staring at her, eyes narrowed with a curiosity that flickered between amused and cautious, a second glance that she rarely saw in anyone, especially not in strangers thrown together by circumstance.

Emma's fingers twitched, hesitating over her notebook, yet she hesitated only for a moment before flipping it open to reveal her latest drawings. Her sketches were meticulous, not the hurried doodles one might expect from nervousness but detailed architectural renderings—blueprints of the train car itself. She had sketched emergency exits, security cameras, even the placement of staff, all with an unerring precision. It was a strange choice for someone seemingly so composed, and Liam's eyes flicked from her face to her sketches, suspicion sparking in his gaze.

"You're an artist?" he finally asked, voice low but edged with something that sounded more like intrigue than mere politeness.

Emma offered a slight shrug, closing her sketchbook gently.

"Not exactly. I draw to clear my mind, that's all. It

helps me focus, especially in situations like this."

Her voice was steady, but beneath it was a flicker of defiance—she wasn't about to reveal too much, not yet.

Liam nodded, but there was an unspoken questions hanging between them, thick as the rain beating softly against the window.

Later that night, as the carriage grew colder and the landscape blurred into shadows, Emma caught Liam speaking quietly into his phone. She was half buried in her coat, her sketchbook on her knees, pretending to be absorbed in her notes. But her eyes flicked over him, catching the subtle tension in his posture.

She listened, catching snippets of Arabic, a language that didn't belong to her region, yet sounded familiar in the strange, tense air of the train. Liam's voice was hushed but urgent, phrases like "the package" and "the next stop" slipping out. When he hung up, he looked around, trying to mask his own unease.

Emma's stomach clenched. Her grandmother's letter had mentioned a "treasure," something hidden, secret. What if Liam was involved in the same dangerous game? Her thoughts spun as her mind raced through every word her grandmother had written, every warning embedded within. She thought about her sketches—the ones she drew not as art but as codes, blueprints for something much bigger. Could Liam know? Was he part of this tangled web? Her heart pounded in her chest with the weight of unspoken truths, and suddenly, the space between them seemed charged with more than just the delay.

As dawn approached, the train's movement was sluggish, and the atmosphere grew more oppressive. Emma kept her gaze fixed on the window, watching the bleak landscape blur into a grey wash, unsure of what dangers lurked just beyond the horizon.

Liam leaned closer, voice lowered so only she could hear.

"We're not just stuck because of weather," he said quietly. "There's more to this. I think someone's been watching us." He paused, eyes narrowing as he studied her. "The sketches—you're hiding something, aren't you?"

Emma's breath hitched. The secret she carried was heavier than any sketch she'd ever made. She hesitated for a heartbeat before she finally nodded, voice grim.

"My real name isn't Emma Clarke. I used to be an investigator—an insurance investigator, really. I was tracking art fraud, stolen pieces from WWII, and my grandmother's letters… they're more than just mysterious notes." Her eyes held Liam's, a mix of fear and resolve. "I've spent years trying to find evidence that could bring down a network of art thieves. The treasure isn't gold or jewels. It's documents—proof of a crime that reaches deep into history and right into the present day."

Liam listened intently, a flicker of understanding crossing his face. His own secrets were just beneath the surface—disguised as a travel writer, but actually an undercover operative working for Interpol, hunting down a ring of stolen art shipping through the railway network. The pieces of her story fit with his, and now they understood that their paths had crossed involuntarily. Neither of them said much for a while, the silence heavy with the weight of their revelations.

Outside, the storm still raged, a metaphor for the chaos enveloping their lives, doubts creeping in like shadows in the dark.

The train lurched again as it hit an obstacle. Inside, Emma's fingers brushed her sketches, the blueprints that might someday reveal the secrets she'd been chasing all her life. Meanwhile, Liam's mind spun with the realization—they weren't just passengers. They were targets in a game much larger than themselves. Their journey toward Paris was no longer just about arriving—it was about survival, about unmasking the lies, and uncovering the truth buried beneath layers of deceit. The storm outside was relentless, and inside, so was the quiet storm building between two strangers about to find out just how dangerous their world had become.

3
Unveiling Secrets

The confined space of the train seemed to shrink around Emma as she stared at the faded parchment of her grandmother's letter. Its words, once a mysterious whisper from the past, now echoed with a clarity that sent a shiver down her spine. Her grandmother's mention of a treasure had always felt symbolic, a metaphor for something lost—a family legacy buried beneath layers of secrecy. Yet, in this moment, that metaphor cracked open, revealing something far more tangible: a story of betrayal, resistance, and hidden archives. Emma's pulse quickened; her brush with the past was no longer a faint curiosity but a dangerous pursuit pulling her into shadows she'd only glimpsed before.

Across from her, Liam watched her with cautious eyes. The flickering of the sparse overhead light cast shadows across his face, highlighting the weariness etched into his features. The world outside the window was a blur—a smear of darkness punctuated by distant city lights—yet inside, tension simmered between them, thick and palpable. Liam sensed change in Emma; her calm façade was cracking, revealing the fierce determination beneath. For him, every moment of their strangeness felt like a page turning in a story he was only beginning to understand—a story that entwined them more tightly than either had anticipated. Beneath her composed exterior, Emma held a silent vow: to unearth what her grandmother had kept hidden and to find meaning in the chaos surrounding them.

Her true mission became painfully clear as she unfolded her own story—a story she'd guarded for years. She was not just an art restorer; she was an investigator, a seeker of truth in a world where art and deception often blurred. For years, she had scoured auction houses, interrogated shady dealers, and followed leads darkened by greed and corruption. Her grandmother's cryptic references to a hidden archive suddenly made sense. That treasure was more than a relic or a piece of stolen art—it was evidence of a vast network that had operated during the war, hiding stolen masterpieces and concealing the truth. This mission wasn't just about history; it was about justice, about exposing the lies that had shadowed her family for generations.

As Emma's revelation settled over her, Liam's own

cover story began to unravel in his mind. His latest case, he realized, had never been about mere smuggling routes or stolen artifacts. It was about a web—one that linked Emma's investigations to his own covert work for Interpol. Their paths, once apart and seemingly unrelated, now exploded into focus. Liam had been working undercover, infiltrating illegal networks that trafficked not just art but lives. His panic attacks, which had haunted him for months, weren't just symptoms of trauma—they were alarm bells warning him he was in too deep. And now, somehow, Emma's story was threading into his own, pulling him closer to a revelation that could threaten everything they'd fought for.

In that cramped train carriage, arrays of clues aligned with relentless precision. Emma's sketches of hidden compartments and Liam's whispered phone conversations painted a portrait of two intersecting worlds—two investigations that had become one. Both of them, unwittingly, had stumbled into a trap: the delays, the unwelcome stops—they weren't accidents. Someone was watching. Someone wanted to silence them before they could expose the truth. Their shared realization deepened the stakes, transforming their fragile alliance into a battle against unseen enemies. The train, once a vehicle for travel, had become a prison—and time was running out.

Confusion brewed as Emma and Liam pieced through these new truths. Every passenger, every familiar face aboard the train, suddenly shimmered with suspicion. The friendly conductor, who smiled so politely and handed out blankets, could just as easily be a shadow agent, slipping a drug into their coffee. The elderly French couple, who exchanged warm greetings and shared stories, carried secrets deeper than words. Even the seemingly innocuous businessman who lent Liam his phone charger might have been an operative, an unwitting pawn in a well-placed game of deception. Emma's mind raced, each detail whispering warnings that their safety was fragile. They needed to move, and fast, yet the knowledge that their phones had been cloned—every text, every call made them feel helpless, vulnerable shadows in a game they couldn't even see.

Driven by a mixture of fear and defiance, Emma clutched her bag, knowing that the apartment in Montmartre awaited—a hideaway hinted at in her grandmother's letters, where secrets and truths intertwined within darkened corridors and hidden chambers. That hidden fortress, built by her grandmother during her resistance days, was no mere refuge; it was a vault of evidence. Here lay the records that could dismantle the entire criminal operation, and reveal the truth about her family's involvement in crimes stretching back decades. Yet, with every passing minute, Emma understood that they weren't just chasing relics—they were racing against those who would kill to keep their secrets buried. The train's final stop was approaching, and with it, the moment when everything would come crashing down.

***

The dim lighting of the Montmartre apartment reflected softly on the dust-covered records and faded paintings that lined the walls. Shadows flickered across Liam's face as he stared at the screen of his phone, the flickering glow illuminating the worry etched into his features. In that moment, he knew everything was unraveling faster than he could control. His secret, his other life, was no longer hidden beneath the surface—it was on full display, a fragile paper boat ready to sink beneath the weight of truth. The silence hung heavy, thick enough to choke, as the implications of his covert activities pressed down on him like an iron weight. He had always believed he could keep both worlds separate, but now, they were crashing into each other with relentless force.

Memories of late-night stakeouts, whispered conversations on dark train platforms, and hurried exchanges flashed through his mind. For years, he'd woven a tapestry of lies—disguises, false identities, debts paid in shadow—and this clandestine existence had become as familiar as breathing. Yet, tonight, everything teetered on the brink. Emma's piercing gaze, her unyielding resolve, and her unspoken questions made him feel exposed in ways he'd never experienced before. Could she sense the truth? Did her intuition detect the fox hiding behind the calm veneer? His heart pounded fiercely, each beat echoing the real risk: if she uncovered his secret, both their lives would be irrevocably changed. Still, he couldn't abandon her now—his instincts screamed that revealing everything might be the only way to save them both from impending destruction.

Across the room, Emma's breath caught as she watched him, her mind racing. Liam's voice had sounded strange earlier, clipped and cautious, like he was hiding something. Her ears had picked up snippets—words like "package" and "deadline"—foreign terms spoken with an urgency that didn't belong to a travel writer. She had dismissed it at first, attributing it to stress or miscommunication, but the more she watched him, the more she sensed that he wasn't merely an ordinary man caught in a string of train delays. The sketches she had seen him scribble earlier in the dead of night now seemed even more sinister in their detailed accuracy—precise notes on security cameras, known escape routes, a meticulous map of the train's weaknesses. Her instincts told her that Liam was not just a traveler—he was involved in something far darker than either of them had anticipated.

Then came the call—an unsettling moment when Liam's phone buzzed sharply in the quiet. He answered quickly, the voice on the other end low and hurried. Emma's ears strained to catch the words. She heard snippets—"the package," "urgent," "tomorrow." His eyes flickered with alarm, and he excused himself hurriedly, leaving her alone in the shadowed room. Emma's grip tightened on her sketchpad, her mind spiraling with questions. Could Liam be part of the same network she was hunting? Was this delay part of a cunning trap or merely bad luck? The letter from her grandmother suddenly felt heavier than ever, a cryptic clue in a web of lies and danger. She felt her stomach tighten, her mind racing to piece together what little she knew about Liam—the man she'd come to trust, yet now questioned more than she'd ever admit aloud.

As night deepened, unease settled over the apartment like thick fog. Emma moved silently, her fingers trembling as she examined the small stack of documents she had secretly hidden in her coat pocket. The pieces aligned with disturbing clarity—Liam's real identity, his undercover role, his connection to international smuggling rings that trafficked stolen art along covert rail routes. Her heart pounded fiercely—her entire mission, her legacy, and perhaps her life, depended on whether she could trust this man or whether he was just another pawn sent to deceive her. Every minute stretched longer, each heartbeat a reminder that they were no longer two strangers lost in Paris but two hunted souls caught in a dangerous game. The walls seemed to close in, and outside, the city of lights blazed indifferent to the storm of secrets brewing inside.

***

The small, crumpled piece of paper trembled in Emma's trembling fingers, yellowed with age yet resilient against the years. It was tucked carefully inside her grandmother's old leather-bound diary, a fragile link to a past she was only beginning to understand. The thick scent of dust and faded ink filled the air as she unrolled the letter, its edges torn from years of being hidden away. Every word seemed to pulse with silent urgency, whispering secrets that had been buried in the shadows of history. Emma's eyes scanned the handwriting, trembling as she realized it was written in her grandmother's delicate script, each letter a piece of a puzzle she didn't yet know how to assemble.

She sat silently in the dim light of the Montmartre apartment, surrounded by relics of her family's past—paintings, old photographs, and the faint echo of footsteps long gone. The letter's contents hinted at a clandestine meeting, a secret treasure concealed beneath the very streets they had walked so many times without knowing. Her heart pounded as the implications sank deeper: this wasn't just about some lost relic; it was about reconnecting with her grandmother's hidden life, a web of deception spun during wartime and kept alive through decades. Emma could feel the weight of history pressing down on her, the ghosts of the past whispering in her ear, urging her to uncover what had been deliberately concealed.

Every word, every smudge of ink, seemed to beckon her closer to truths buried beneath layers of lies and silence and stained with the blood of secrets kept too long.

On the smooth wooden table lay an old photograph, slightly faded and worn at the edges. It showed her grandmother, Margot, young and fierce, standing beside a narrow alleyway in Montmartre, her face set with determination. On the back, in hurried script, a single word: "Read."

Emma's fingers brushed over it, trembling with anticipation. The letter had led her here, to a city filled with stories long suppressed—stories that now threatened to explode into her life. As she traced her grandmother's image, Emma felt a shiver run through her body. This was no ordinary inheritance. It was a dangerous inheritance—a chain of lies that stretched across generations, with her grandmother at its center. Emma knew that finding the truth would mean stepping into a world filled with shadows and jeopardy, risking everything she'd left behind. And yet, the pull to solve the mystery, to connect the dots, was stronger than ever, propelling her into a night she might never escape.

Suddenly, her phone buzzed, slicing through the silence like a dagger. Emma's heart leapt; her hand shot out instinctively. The screen illuminated a message from an unknown number:

"They're watching you. Trust no one."

Instantly, her mind raced—the timing was too perfect. Was it a warning? Or a trap? Her pulse quickened as the weight of suspicion pressed down. She remembered Liam's words about the danger he'd sensed on the train, the cryptic conversations he'd overheard in the night. Was he involved in this? Or was she? Every thought was a whirl of doubt and fear, spiraling toward an inevitable conclusion. The shadows in the room seemed to deepen, the faintest whisper of movement catching her eye. She clasped the letter tightly, feeling the fragile paper's cold touch anchoring her to reality amid the storm of questions. Somewhere in the darkness, unseen eyes watched her, waiting for her next move—an unspoken menace lurking just beyond her sight. Emma knew she could no longer hide from the truth. It was time to follow the letter's lead—into the depths of Montmartre, into the heart of mystery, and perhaps, into mortal danger.

4
Revelations in the Night

The dim glow of a streetlamp cast flickering shadows across the uneven cobblestones of Montmartre. Emma moved quietly, her breath shallow, her heart pounding like a distant drum. Every step brought her closer to the apartment her grandmother had once whispered about in hushed tones—hidden behind a false wall, secret tunnels that winded through the old stone beneath her. She clutching a small, worn leather case that contained the evidence her grandmother had sworn was the truth—and her salvation. The air was thick with anticipation, each creak of the floorboards beneath her feet feeling like a heartbeat echoing through the silence.

Inside the apartment, darkness embraced her like an old friend. Flickering flashlight in hand, Emma navigated the cluttered space, her eyes darting across the dense tapestry of photographs, handwritten notes, and maps plastered on peeling walls. She sensed someone watching, a shadow lurking just beyond the fragile edge of her vision. Every nerve was alert, every molecule alive with the awareness of danger lurking behind the seemingly still silence.

This was no ordinary hideout—it was a fortress, built over decades by a woman who knew how to cover her tracks, and Emma was now walking directly into her grandmother's web of secrets.

Suddenly, a faint click echoed through the room—a sound that sliced through the silence like a knife. Emma froze, heartbeat hammering against her ribcage. From the darkness, a figure stepped forward, calm and deliberate. Margot Dubois.

Emma felt a chill as the realization set in: her grandmother was alive, and she had been waiting all along. Margot's eyes gleamed with a cold mixture of pride and menace, her lips curling into a faint, knowing smile.

"You've come far, Emma," she whispered softly, voice smooth as silk but sharp as steel. "But you're not yet ready to see the whole picture. Not until I show you what I've protected all these years."

Emma's mind raced, trying to process this revelation. Margot's face was a relic of resistance and betrayal, a woman who had danced through history's shadows without ever losing her grip.

"Why?" Emma managed to whisper, her voice trembling. "Why hide all of this from me?"

Her grandmother's smile widened, tragic and triumphant all at once.

"Because I needed to keep you safe," she said. "From them—and from yourself. The truth is dangerous, Emma. Much more than you realize."

The room suddenly seemed to close in, the weight of history pressing down on Emma's shoulders. Draped over the tables were records, photographs, and artifacts—evidence of decades of hidden crimes, meticulously preserved and long concealed.

She reached out, fingers trembling, and brushed against a leather-bound journal. The pages within detailed transactions, secret meetings, and names—powerful figures who had used Emma's ancestors and her grandmother's own actions as pawns in a larger game. The puzzle pieces clicked into place: this wasn't just her family's secret, it was a network built on lies, theft, and bloodshed.

Margot's voice broke the heavy silence again, laden with finality.

"You've been searching for something that could topple empires, Emma. The paintings, the records—they're just the surface. The real treasure is what lies beneath, in these documents. Every deal, every betrayal, every stolen piece—exposed. If you dare to reveal these secrets, it could destroy everything, everyone. Or it could finally set things right."

Emma's mind spun. Her mission had always been driven by the desire for truth, but now it unveiled itself as a reckoning—one that threatened their last fragile ties and her understanding of her entire history. She looked at her grandmother, the woman she had admired, betrayed by her own past, cloaked in shadows that had stretched across generations. The stakes had never been higher. With a heavy breath, Emma clenched her fists, knowing that the discovery could change everything—and that time was running out.

***

In the dim light of the Montmartre apartment, Emma's heart hammered against her ribs like a prisoner desperate for release. Her fingers trembled as she sifted through the faded documents hidden beneath a loose brick in the wall. They were brittle, yellowed with age but packed with secrets—files detailing stolen artworks, coded transactions, and names that echoed the dark history of her family.

For years, she had suspected that her grandmother's mysterious past was more than just whispers and half-told stories, but now, with these records in her hands, the truth shivered to life before her eyes. This was the real treasure—the evidence that could finally expose the sprawling web of art thieves, Nazi collaborators, and the illicit dealers who had thrived in shadows for decades.

Meanwhile, Liam stood quietly near the doorway, watching Emma with a mixture of awe and unease. His mind was racing, piecing together the fragments of his own hidden world. His cover as a travel writer had shielded him from suspicion long enough, but here, amid the secrets of Montmartre, his false persona was cracking. His role in Interpol was more than just clandestine; it was a dangerous dance on a wire stretched tight over a pit of betrayal. Every word spoken, every glance exchanged, felt laden with the weight of their shared danger. Liam knew that their discovery was just the beginning—and that the shadows lurking beneath the city's romantic veneer had already cast their long, dark net over them.

Then, Emma's voice broke the silence, trembling yet resolute.

"This... this is what my grandmother risked everything to hide. These records aren't just dates and names—they're a map of everything she fought against. The art ring, the Nazi connections, all of it. If we can get this out into the open, we could bring down years of corruption, restore what was stolen... and finally unravel the lie that has haunted my family for generations."

Liam stepped closer, his jaw clenched.

"And what's the plan now? We can't stay here indefinitely. Margot might have someone watching this apartment, waiting for us to make a move."

The words hung heavy in the air, thick with unspoken fears that a confrontation was imminent. The shadows seemed to creep closer, eager to hide secrets better left buried.

Suddenly, a faint movement from the hallway—a whisper of footsteps—made both of them freeze. Emma's eyes widened, scanning the doorway where a shadow flickered—a figure lurking just beyond the faint glow of a streetlight filtering through the window. Her breath caught in her throat. Liam instinctively reached for his phone, but the screen remained dark—a cruel reminder that their communications had been compromised. Panic prickled along her skin, but she steadied herself.

"They know we've found something," she whispered, voice trembling with a mixture of fear and determination. "Margot's empire is wider than we thought. We're running out of time."

For a moment, their worlds teetered on the edge of chaos—each heartbeat a drumbeat in a perilous symphony, signaling that the hour of reckoning was near, and the battle for justice was about to explode into the open.

***

The train trembled beneath them as the storm's fury pressed against the windows. Shadows flickered irregularly, casting distorted shapes that danced across Emma's anxious face. Her fingers tightened on her coat, each breath she took muddled with the scent of damp fabric and compounded dread. It was as if the night had become a labyrinth, spiraling toward an unknown destination, every minute stretching longer than the last.

Liam sat across from her, his jaw clenched with the weight of secrets he refused to voice. The flickering light revealed the tense lines carved into his face, echoes of memories he wished to forget. His eyes flitted toward Emma, noticing the way her hands trembled as she sketched something hurriedly in a worn notebook. In that brief moment, he sensed a strange kinship—a shared burden beneath their different façades—though neither dared admit it aloud.

As the seconds stretched into minutes, Emma's pencil traced rapid, intricate lines—faint outlines of a building, a train station, hidden compartments. Her hands moved with purpose, betraying a calm exterior she desperately fought to maintain. Liam couldn't help but lean forward, eyes narrowing as he watched her work. There was an intensity in her strokes; it felt as if she was mapping out not just architecture, but her own fragile psyche, trying to hold herself together amid chaos.

In the quiet moments that followed, Emma finally lowered her pencil, her gaze fixed on the sketches. She whispered softly, almost to herself, about necessity—the need for control in a world gone adrift. Liam's gaze lingered longer this time, reading the lines as silent words, sensing they told stories far deeper than the surface. Outside, the storm raged on, a primal force echoing their own turbulent secrets, threatening to tear apart the thin veneer of civility they desperately clung to.

Later that night, during a lull in their turbulent journey, Emma noticed Liam on his phone, speaking softly in a language that wasn't familiar—Arabic, perhaps, or something close enough to stir her suspicion. She pretended to focus on her sketches, but the words caught her ear as she sat in the dim glow of the overhead light. Words like package and tomorrow's deadline floated through her mind like a puzzle piece falling into place. Her heart thudded uncomfortably, realizing the puzzle was bigger—more dangerous—than she had initially thought.

Her grandmother's letter floated in her mind, suddenly feeling heavy and ominous, the possibility of coincidence dissolving into real dread. What if the missing treasure wasn't just a legend, but a key to something far darker? She observed Liam, whose face was tense, exposing flashes of concealed burden—secrets masked behind her own trembling silence. The train, once a simple vessel of travel, now seemed like a stage set for something sinister, its calm cracked beneath the storm's relentless assault.

That moment marked a turning point—an unspoken realization settled between them. Emma questioned everything she thought she knew, and Liam, caught in his own web of deception, wondered if he'd find salvation in truth or be swallowed by it. As the rain battered the carriage's metal shell and thunder rolled in the distance, they sat captured in a silence thick with anticipation and danger, each weighing whether they could trust the shadows hiding within this night of chaos. The weight of secrets pressed down, threatening to expose them in the darkness before dawn, and neither knew what—or who—would emerge from the shadows when the storm finally broke.

5
Danger Looms

The train's rhythmic clatter echoed softly through the carriage, a sound that seemed strangely mundane considering the weight of what was at stake. Emma sat near the window, her eyes fixed on the blurred landscape rushing past, but her mind was elsewhere—focused on the subtle cues around her. Every passenger seemed wrapped in their own world, yet Emma knew that covert operatives could be hiding behind any of those unassuming faces. Her senses had sharpened over years in investigations, but now, amid the quiet hum of the train, the challenge felt even more daunting. She kept her posture relaxed, but her fingers twitched involuntarily, ready to reach for her bag if needed. One of her primary missions was to decipher the unspoken tension in these seconds, to suss out the dangerous from the innocent in this moving microcosm of Europe's hidden shadows.

Across the aisle, Liam watched the people with a more casual gaze, but his own instincts hummed softly beneath the surface. His days of war reporting had taught him to read faces and body language like a language itself, picking out the lies buried behind polite smiles or the nervous tic that betrayed a guilty conscience. He sensed that some here weren't simply travelers passing through; they were players in a game much bigger than a delayed train. The quiet lady clutching her purse, the man reading a newspaper with meticulous focus—each detail could be a cipher to crack. Liam leaned back subtly, eyes narrowing as he scanned their expressions, searching for that flicker, that hesitation that might reveal someone working against them. Their safety depended on these small glimpses, on catching whispers in a crowded carriage where every word could be a trap or a plea for help.

Suddenly, the carriage dipped as the train slowed, an ominous groan from beneath their feet announcing another halt. Emma's stomach clenched; the delay wasn't just a matter of weather anymore. The storm had turned into a barricade, blocking their escape route. But beneath her apprehension lurked something else—an instinct that told her this wasn't simply bad luck. She remembered her grandmother's words: "Trust no one. Watch everyone." Those words echoed in her mind as she watched passengers shift uneasily, eyes cast downward or greeting each other with lingering, lingering glances. She noticed the elderly French couple whispering hurriedly behind their hands, whispering words she couldn't catch. Even the helpful conductor, with his chipped smile and cheerful tone, seemed orchestrated—how much of his pleasantness was genuine? Emma tightened her grip on her bag, feeling the weight of suspicion settle like a cloak around her shoulders. Somewhere in this carriage was a threat, hidden among those who appeared harmless, and she had to find it before it was too late.

***

The train carriage hummed softly, a familiar drone that masked the growing pulses of dread pounding in Emma's chest. Her fingertips trembled as she stared at her phone, dead and unresponsive, and a cold sweat broke out across her forehead. Moments ago, she had spoken to Liam, their voices muffled by the crackling static, but suddenly, her device had gone dark—completely compromised. It was as if the silence itself had devoured the connection, erasing moments of reassurance just as they'd needed it most.

Every beep, every swipe now felt like a step closer to the danger that lurked just beyond the curve of her peripheral vision. Emma knew her phone wasn't just a tool anymore; it was a fragile lifeline, and now it was broken, potentially infiltrated, and entirely at the mercy of unseen enemies. Her heart hammered against her ribs, a persistent drumbeat of fear that refused to quiet down.

From across the aisle, Liam watched her with cautious eyes. His brow furrowed as his own phone flashed an ominous message:

'Device Disabled.'

The realization hit him hard—these weren't ordinary tech issues. Someone had accessed their devices, infiltrated their digital defenses, and rendered them useless. It was no coincidence. They had been careless for a moment, lulled into a false sense of security amid the chaos of the delays and the shadows of distrust that crept into their minds. Now, that carelessness threatened everything. Their plans to communicate, to coordinate their next moves, were suddenly sabotaged. Liam's jaw tightened as he clenched his fists. They had just moved past the point of simple caution; they were now completely exposed, vulnerable to a network of silent predators lurking inside the very devices meant to protect them.

Emma's eyes darted around the carriage, searching for any sign of the operators who might have been watching. She remembered the conductor's friendly smile, the elderly couple's warm chatter, the business-man's casual courtesy—all of it felt like a mask now. The realization coiled in her stomach: everyone on this train could be working for them, or against them. The friendly face offering assistance might have been a pawn in an intricate game. Her mind raced back to Emma's past—her days as an investigator had often involved understanding the psychology of deception, but here she was, a participant in its most danger-ous form. Her fingers tapped anxiously at her lap, in-stinctively trying to reboot her phone, but the screen remained blank. She understood now. Whoever had done this knew everything—every plan, every move, every piece of information stored in their pockets, in their lives, in their very phones.

The flickering overhead lights cast shadows that

danced along the walls, lengthening with every passing second. Emma whispered softly, more to herself than anyone else:

"They're inside."

The words hung heavy in the confined space.

Liam leaned closer, his voice husky but deliberate.

"Can we try to switch devices? Or does that make things worse?"

Emma shook her head, her mind racing through options. The doors to the carriage rattled faintly, the sounds of the station beyond. Outside, rain poured down in sheets, a relentless curtain that mocked any hope of escape. Whoever had infiltrated their phones was likely listening. Listening and waiting to strike at any moment. Their enemy knew their every move, every word, every hesitation. It was the kind of threat that made eyes dart and hearts race, as if unseen hands now gripped their fates in a tightening fist.

The realization was like a weight pressed against Emma's chest, squeezing the breath from her lungs. Their long-standing assumptions about safety on this journey dissolved in a single moment. No one could be trusted—not even the friendly staff or the fellow passengers who had shared their stories and coffee. The technology that had once seemed so reliable now betrayed them, offering the enemy a perfect loophole. Emma's mind flashed back to recent conversations, whispered secrets she'd thought safe—her grandmother's notes, Liam's covert calls, the sketches she'd hidden in her bag. The cold truth settled in: their compromised phones meant everything was exposed, every secret at risk of being leaked to those who would do anything to silence them.

They had been betrayed, not by a foe in the shadows but by the very tools themselves, which now turned into weapons aimed directly at their vulnerabilities.

In the cramped silence that followed, Emma felt a prickling at the back of her neck. A faint, almost imperceptible crackle seeped through her earpiece—the only remaining link to Liam. Frantic, she reached up, trying to hear him more clearly, but the line was dead. For a moment, everything seemed frozen in time: the rain's rhythm on the roof, the muted hum of the carriage, her racing thoughts. Then, slowly, a figure moved through the shadows—a figure she hadn't noticed before. It was the conductor, walking deliberately toward them with a subtle yet calculated stride.

His eyes lingered just a fraction too long. Was he part of this web? Her mind spun as she watched him, recalling how his grip on the coffee service had seemed too tight, how his smiles never quite reached his eyes. Suddenly, the darkness outside the carriage felt oppressive, closing in like the walls of a trap. Emma's knuckles whitened around her seat armrest. She knew, with grim certainty, that her device wasn't just compromised; it had been weaponized. And if her phone could be hacked and monitored, so could her mind, her movements, everything she was trying to protect. The game was now about survival, played with invisible strings pulling tight, and the stakes had never been higher.

***

The narrow alleyways of Montmartre seem to twist and turn like a labyrinth, the shadows cast by old, bending trees causing flickering patches of darkness on the cobblestones. Emma moved cautiously, her eyes scanning the quiet streets, feeling the weight of her secret buried beneath layers of dust and time. She held a small leather-bound notebook close, the faint glow of a distant streetlamp illuminating the faded sketches drawn in hurried strokes—details that others wouldn't notice, but she knew lay at the heart of her mission. Every step she took brought her closer to the apartment her grandmother had once called her refuge, yet tonight, it seemed more like a fortress.

The building itself was unassuming from the outside—a small, weathered stone façade with a forgotten plaque and a creaky wooden door. Emma's fingers trembled as she reached into her coat pocket, feeling the cold metal of the tiny key her grandmother had left her. It had been passed down through generations of secretive women, each adding their own layer of protection and concealment. The air was thick with anticipation, a strange lull that hung heavy like a storm about to break. She hesitated only a moment before turning the key, the door creaking open with a groan that echoed softly into the silence beyond.

Inside, the apartment was a time capsule. Dust

motes floated lazily in the rare pockets of moonlight that seeped through the partially boarded windows. The walls were lined with peeling wallpaper, torn in places to reveal faded murals beneath—hidden stories of a life lived in shadows. Emma stepped carefully over scattered papers, old photographs, and discarded pieces of art that seemed to whisper secrets of decades long gone. As she moved deeper into the darkness, her eyes caught sight of a narrow staircase leading downward, spiraling into darkness. This was her grandmother's secret sanctum—the underground chambers where stories of resistance, betrayal, and stolen gold once intertwined.

Her heartbeat quickened as the faint scent of old paper and damp stone filled her senses. Every creak of the settling building sounded amplified, a reminder that she was trespassing into a space long forgotten. Emma reached the bottom of the staircase and paused, her hand brushing along the cold brick wall. The small flashlight she carried revealed a hidden door, concealed behind a false wall that she quickly recognized from her grandmother's hurried sketches. With a calculated breath, she pushed aside the crumbling bricks, revealing a narrow passageway that led into the secret rooms beneath Montmartre—the place where her grandmother's past and her present collided.

The air grew colder as Emma stepped forward, her footsteps echoing softly. The corridor opened into a larger space lit by faint candle stubs and the flickering glow of distant flames. Shelves crammed with dusty files, art catalogs, and strange gadgets lined the walls. Here, in this hidden fortress, Emma sensed the weight of centuries—her ancestors' whispers embedded in every stone and shadow. Carefully, she moved toward a battered wooden table cluttered with faded records and photographs. Her fingers trembled as she touched a black-and-white photo of a young woman—her grandmother—smiling amidst chaos. Beneath it, a ledger detailed illicit transactions, smuggling routes, and secret deals. The clues had been waiting all along, silent witnesses to a web of deception that now threatened to unravel everything.

Suddenly, a faint noise made her freeze. From the shadows emerged a dark silhouette—boots heavy on stone, slow and deliberate. Emma's breath caught as she recognized the figure's posture—the way they held themselves, the faint glint of a weapon at their side. Every instinct sharpened. As the figure drew closer, Emma instinctively backed into a corner, clutching her notebook tight. The face came into focus—a stranger's, yet they moved with the familiarity of someone who belonged here, someone who knew these depths intimately. She realized, with a sinking feeling, that she wasn't alone in this darkness. Danger lurked behind every obscure corner—silent, patient, waiting to strike.

As tension hung thick in the air, Emma's mind raced. Was this person a thief? An investigator like herself? Or worse, someone sent to silence her forever? Her gaze darted around, searching for any hidden escape or tool that might turn the tide in her favor. Suddenly, the stranger spoke in a low, gravelly voice, startling her.

"You shouldn't be here."

The words were simple, but their tone carried an ominous weight, as if the shadows themselves agreed. Everything from her grandmother's records, the secret passages, and her own trembling hope converged into this moment. With her heart pounding in her ears, Emma realized she had crossed a line—into a world where betrayal, secrets, and death danced close, and there was no turning back now.

6
Betrayal and Deception

The train lurched suddenly, metal groaning under the strain as another curve was taken too sharply. Emma's heart hammered in her chest, but she kept her eyes fixed on the window, pretending calmness she didn't feel. Outside, the city's lights flickered like distant flames fading into the dark, an unspoken promise of safety she feared might be a lie.

Liam leaned back in his seat, watching her with guarded curiosity, his own nerves coiled tight beneath his composed exterior. Neither of them knew that the peril encroaching upon them was far more than the violent weather—they were caught in a web spun long before they boarded this train, and now, it was tightening around their ankles.

The small, battered phone in Liam's hand buzzed silently, its screen flashing with a message he deliberately ignored. His mind was racing, knowing that every word, every call could be shadowed, listened to by unseen eyes. Emma shifted in her seat, her fingers trembling as she clutched the small leather notebook filled with sketches and notes. The ink had smudged from her sweat, but the drawings of the train's layout and security measures were precise—she knew these details wouldn't just be idle doodles. Liam's gaze flickered to her, sensing her tension, yet saying nothing as he watched the door for any sign of danger.

Suddenly, the train slowed, a rough jolt that made both of them sit upright. The lights flickered overhead, casting shadows that danced like specters across the carriage. Emma tensed, remembering the strange glint she'd seen in the conductor's eyes earlier that day. He had been overly accommodating, too eager to keep them comfortable, as if hinting at something behind the friendly facade. Liam's jaw tightened; he recognized the trap. His instincts whispered that this delay was no accident. The storm's fury was merely a distraction—these delays, the tangled web of minor technical faults and smoke screens—they were all part of a larger scheme, one that they had unwittingly stepped into. And whatever was waiting in Paris might already be closing in.

In the cabin's dim glow, Emma's eyes flicked toward her sketches again. Her hand instinctively traced the lines of an emergency exit, a small detail she'd noted earlier. Each line felt like a breadcrumb, a clue in a puzzle designed to keep them alive—or to eliminate them. Liam noticed her concentration and leaned closer, lowering his voice.

"You're drawing more than comfort doodles," he murmured.

Her shoulders tense, Emma hesitated before answering.

"It's just security," she replied swiftly, too quickly.

But he wasn't convinced. In his line of work, the subtle signs always pointed to something hidden beneath the surface. They both knew they were walking through a minefield—a single step could trigger an explosion they wouldn't survive.

Then came the whisper of voices, faint but distinct, emanating from the phone in Liam's hand. His eyes widened as he silently read the messages that flickered onto the screen—messages that revealed more than mere conversation. He had been quietly exchanging code with an unknown contact, details carefully encrypted but unmistakably urgent. His cover was slipping. The phrase "the package," "tomorrow's deadline,"—these words sent icy spikes down his spine. Emma noticed the sudden change in his demeanor and stiffened. A terrible realization dawned: their chase through the shadows of Paris was not just an investigation anymore; it had become a race against unseen enemies who knew everything about them. Everything they thought they understood was a lie wrapped in deception.

Outside, the storm continued its relentless assault, battering the carriage like a vengeful beast. Inside, the tension was sticky, thick enough to cut with a blade. Emma's mind raced to connect the dots—her grandmother's letter, the stolen art, the shadowy figure Liam was talking to—everything pointed to a dangerous conspiracy that reached into the darkest corners of history. Her secret past as an investigator surfaced with urgent clarity—this wasn't just about stolen paintings or hidden treasures. It was about enemies who would kill to keep their secrets buried, enemies who had been watching her family for decades. With a sense of rising dread, Emma realized that her plan to stay hidden was impossible now. She was in too deep, and the false escape they had hoped for was nothing more than a prelude to the real battle lying ahead.

*****

The train's sudden screeching halt jolted Emma upright, her heart pounding in tandem with the rail beneath her. Outside the window, the flickering orange glow of scattered streetlights cast long shadows over the deserted tracks. The truth hit her like a cold punch—this delay wasn't natural. Someone had orchestrated it. She stared at Liam, whose normally steady eyes now darted with a flicker of suspicion. Every nerve in her body tensed as the murmur of whispered conversations and distant footsteps echoed in the silence.

As the minutes stretched into an agonizing eternity, Emma's fingers brushed her pocket, feeling the reassuring weight of the hidden documents. Her mind raced, piecing together what she knew—her grandmother's secrets, the stolen art, the danger lurking in every shadow. Liam, meanwhile, was unusually silent, eyes scanning the darkened corridor of the carriage as if expecting an ambush. Suddenly, the clatter of footsteps grew louder—approaching swiftly. Emma's breath hitched. They weren't alone anymore.

From the darkness, a figure emerged—calm but commanding. It was Margot, her grandmother's elusive voice disguised behind a leather mask of coldness.

"You think this is a coincidence?" she whispered, voice sharp as a blade. "The delays? The interruptions? It's all part of the plan."

Emma felt a shiver run down her spine, her mind grappling with the betrayal. Margot's eyes flicked over Liam, then settled on Emma, a cruel smile curling the corners of her mouth.

"You were meant to be caught. Just like the rest of them."

The realization hit with brutal clarity—Margot hadn't just been hiding; she had been orchestrating from the shadows all along. Emma's world teetered on the edge of collapse as the connections she fought so desperately to uncover suddenly snapped into place. Liam's calm facade cracked for a split second, revealing a flicker of anger and desperation. Emma clutched her notes tightly, knowing that their only chance was to outwit her grandmother, to turn her own treachery against her. But Margot's confidence was unshakable, her presence enveloping the carriage like a storm ready to break.

Without warning, a door slammed open, and a chorus of footsteps stormed the carriage—police, or so it seemed. They burst in, guns drawn, faces grim. Emma's heart hammered louder as she stared at Liam, searching his expression. Was he in on this? The answer flickered in his eyes—he was fighting his own battle, caught just as deep. Margot, however, refused to surrender. With a flick of her hand, she revealed a small, encrypted device, clutched tightly in her palm.

"Your interloper tricks won't save you," she hissed. "I've planned too long for this moment."

Emma's gaze darted to Liam, who suddenly tensed. She saw the flicker of a hidden oath in his eyes—trust no one, especially not her supposed allies.

As the standoff intensified and sirens blared closer, Emma realized that the battle for both her grandmother's secrets and her life was just beginning. The train — a metal beast trapped in a storm of lies — was heading toward a collision she couldn't yet see. Somewhere inside that chaos, her fight to unveil the truth was about to reach its apex, and the darkness closing in promised to test every ounce of her courage.

***

The Parisian air clung heavily around them as Emma and Liam hurried through the dimly lit streets, shadows flickering from sporadic street lamps. Their so-called escape had been a carefully planned illusion—meant to buy time, to throw off anyone tracking them. But as they turned a corner into a narrow alley, Liam's phone buzzed ominously in his coat pocket. The screen flashed with a message:

They're onto us.

Heartbeats quickened, and Emma's pulse thundered loudly enough to drown out the distant hum of the city. Every step brought them closer to the hidden sanctuary they thought they'd reached, yet a gnawing suspicion told them the trap was closing tight around their ankles.

In the silence that followed, Liam cast a quick glance back, catching a suspicious figure lurking in the shadows. The figure was observing, unmoving, their faces concealed beneath dark hoods. Emma grabbed Liam's arm, desperation flashing in her eyes.

"The apartment, she whispered urgently. It has to be safe. Margot's fortress."

It was a place she had uncovered from her grandmother's cryptic notes—an old, underground complex hidden beneath Montmartre, full of secret passages her grandmother had once used during the war.

But with every step they took towards it, a heaviness settled over her, as if the very ground beneath was turning against them. They knew they weren't exactly running toward sanctuary; more like running into a trap with every breath they took.

Suddenly, Liam's phone erupted with a sharp, shrill ring. The caller ID read Interpol, and Liam hesitated only for a heartbeat before answering, voice tense.

"Liam, listen closely, came the urgent voice of his handler. Your location is compromised. Someone's been feeding info. You're not safe—not in Paris, not anywhere else."

Emma's eyes widened as she grasped the gravity of

what he was saying. This was no longer just an escape; it was a game of deception, a chess match where every pawn was a threat. In that moment, Liam realized the chilling truth: Margot's influence ran far deeper than they'd suspected. Someone within their own ranks had turned traitor, and now, the city that once seemed like their refuge was now a labyrinth of lies and treachery. The realization hit like a fist—every step, every decision, had become a matter of survival, with darkness closing in from all directions.

7
Confronting the Past

The dim light of a flickering bulb cast long shadows across the apartment's cluttered shelves. Old photographs layered with dust, yellowed letters, and fragile documents spilled from leather-bound cases, whispering secrets buried deep. Emma sifted carefully through the scraps, her fingers trembling as she uncovered a leather-bound journal with Margot's name etched into the cover.

Every page she flipped felt like unraveling a tightly wound thread of her own life—a tangled knot of half-truths and long-guarded lies. The air grew thick with suspense, as if the walls themselves were holding their breath, waiting for everything to come crashing down.

As Emma devoured the handwritten entries, the stories of Margot's past unraveled with shocking clarity. She learned that her grandmother had been more than a simple resistance figure. Margot had played both sides—collaborating with the Nazi-looted art circles, then secretly funneling stolen masterpieces through underground networks. Emma could feel her stomach churn—her image of Margot was crumbling.

With each secret record, the illusions she'd carried about her family's integrity shattered into tiny shards, piercing her resolve. She stared at a faded photograph clipped to a page—a young Margot in a revolutionary pose, her eyes burning with conviction, now utterly transformed in her mind into a woman driven by greed and cunning beyond her years.

In the shadows, Liam watched her, sensing her emotional upheaval. He kept quiet, his own mind spinning with the implications. Emma's revelations made his own mission seem even more urgent—this was bigger than stolen art or family secrets. Margot's history was a labyrinth cloaked in deception, and unraveling it might be the key to everything—justice, truth, salvation. Ever so gently, Liam reached out, placing a hand on Emma's shoulder, steadying her as she fought a rising tide of fury and sorrow. The air between them grew thick with unspoken understanding—both of them clutching at fragments of a shared, dangerous truth that bound their future with threads of betrayal and redemption.

She looked up, eyes shimmering with tears, but her voice was steady.

"She used her resistance work as a cover," Emma

whispered. "All these years, she hid her crimes behind the facade of heroism. The treasure—those records—they aren't just paper; they're a map. A map to everything she buried. But why now? Why show me all this?"

Liam studied her carefully.

"Because someone in her circle doesn't want those secrets coming out. I think Margot's been protecting herself all along—maybe even her empire—by hiding everything, counting on time to erase what she did. But now, her past is coming back in full force. And if we're right—whatever she's hiding could topple everything she built."

His voice was barely above a whisper, yet every word hammered in like a command—this was only the beginning of what would be a dangerous, uphill fight.

Suddenly, a faint noise echoed from the corridor—a shuffling, tentative and low. Emma froze, clutching the safety of her coat around her. Liam's instincts sharpened—something was wrong. He stepped toward the door, peering through the crack in the doorframe.

A shadow moved, slight but deliberate. He gestured for Emma to stay back, then edged closer.

His heart pounded in his ears as he pressed his ear against the thin wood. Murmurs—words exchanged in hushed tones that sent a shiver down his spine:

"She's onto us," whispered a voice unmistakably familiar. "We cannot afford any slip-up now. Keep watch."

Liam's pulse quickened. They were not alone in this house. Margot's family secrets extended into the shadows, and someone else had come to close the circle, their motives hidden but deadly.

Emma's breath froze in her chest. Her eyes darted to the door, and her mind raced to connect the pieces. Who was on the other side? Could it be a loyal ally or the very prey they searched for—someone who might expose them all? Every second that ticked by felt like a countdown, each breath a fragile hope that they weren't entirely surrounded. Shadows pressed against the edges of her vision as she grasped Liam's arm, whispering urgently:

"We have to move. Now."

The weight of her past collided with the threat of their present—her family's buried sins ready to explode, and her own survival hanging in the balance. Outside, the dark night pressed against the windows like a witness to the secrets lurking within, waiting to reveal its final hand.

***

The light in the Montmartre apartment flickered faintly, casting shifting shadows across walls lined with dust-covered books, faded photographs, and enigmatic sketches. Emma moved cautiously, her heart pounding like a drumbeat against her ribs, each step echoing in the quiet echo of secrets long buried. Every corner seemed to whisper stories of deception, of hidden truths cloaked beneath layers of time and treachery. As she and Liam narrowed their eyes on the evidence strewn across the room—documents, photographs, and a ledger stained with age—they realized they stood at the edge of something far greater than they had anticipated, a web woven with decades of lies. The air was thick and heavy, as if the very walls remembered the crimes committed here, waiting for someone brave enough to uncover them.

Suddenly, a faint click shattered the silence—a sound too deliberate to be coincidence. Emma froze, instinct kicking in. Her eyes darted around, seeking the source, feeling a sudden disturbance ripple through the room. Liam instinctively reached for his phone, but hesitated; something was wrong. A hidden panel swung open beneath a loose floorboard, revealing a narrow, cloaked passage emerging into darkness. Emma's breath hitched. This was what her grandmother had spoken of in cryptic notes—secret tunnels, constructed by Resistance members during WWII, now a labyrinth of shadows hiding the worst of her family's sins.

Liam stepped forward, voice barely above a whisper:

"This changes everything. We've found what they've been hiding all these years."

Fear and determination flickered within their eyes as they prepared to descend into the unknown, the weight of history pressing down on them.

As they crossed the threshold into the darkness, the air grew colder, and their footsteps echoed like distant thunder. The tunnel's walls were damp, slick with age and neglect, yet lined with symbols and markings etched in hurried strokes—remnants of clandestine meetings and desperate plans. Emma's fingers brushed over a faded inscription, her mind racing through the stories she'd uncovered, now standing in the very arteries of her family's sins. In a small alcove, something glinted faintly—an unassuming leather-bound journal, its pages yellowed with time but filled with meticulous entries. Liam's eyes widened as he carefully opened it, revealing detailed records of stolen artworks, transactions, and names—names that hadn't appeared in the official records.

The truth in her hands was a Pandora's box; the story of her heritage, the dark history she'd spent years trying to deny, now illuminated beneath her fingertips. Emma's breath hitched as she saw her grandmother's handwriting—bold, precise, unwavering. Flipping through the pages, she discovered a map, precisely redrawn, pinpointing a series of hidden locations and secret compartments scattered throughout Montmartre.

She realized then that her entire family legacy was

built upon deception, a fortress of lies concealing a vast network of stolen art, smuggling routes, and betrayals. Her mind spun with the implications; her grandmother's carefully kept secrets tied her past to this clandestine empire that had thrived underground for decades. Every revelation further tightened the coil of dread in her stomach. As Liam examined the documents, a new sense of purpose blossomed.

Together, they held evidence that could topple an empire, expose long-standing corruption, and finally bring justice to those who had been silenced for too long.

Suddenly, a faint sound echoed from the tunnel's natural echoes—a faint rustling, like footsteps approaching from the darkness. Emma's muscles tensed, and she instinctively pressed her back against the wall, clutching the journal tightly.

Liam subtly reached into his coat, senses heightened. They exchanged a quick glance—this was no coincidence. Someone else was here, lurking in shadows. Their eyes darted down the passage, shadows moving just beyond the glow of their flashlights. Emma's heart hammered louder, her mind racing to process the threat. Every second that passed seemed to stretch into an eternity, the silence between each footfall growing more menacing. The hidden passages they'd thought were relics now felt like trapdoors, secrets that could betray them at any moment. The weight of her lineage, the years of family lies, suddenly felt suffocating, pinning her down as the sound of footsteps grew nearer, closing the distance into their very sanctuary.

***

The air in the dimly lit room felt thick, each breath echoing with centuries of secrets. Emma's fingers trembled as she sifted through the faded documents her grandmother had hidden away, discovering meticulous records that told stories she'd never heard. Every page was a puzzle piece—names crossed out, ink smudged, but undeniably connected. Her heart hammered against her ribs, each revelation tugging her deeper into a history tangled with betrayal, heroism, and deceit.

It was as if she had uncovered a map not just of stolen art and hidden rooms, but of her very own bloodline—one she'd only begun to understand. With each discovery, Emma could feel her entire identity shifting. Her grandmother's secret life as a Resistance member was more than a distant echo—it was embedded in her veins. The woman she thought she knew, Margot Dubois, had led a double life that had lasted decades.

The records detailed clandestine meetings, covert transactions, and a series of aliases that shimmered like ghosts from her past. Emma stared at her reflection in the faded glass of a small framed photograph; suddenly, her calm exterior masked a tumult of questions. How much of her childhood had been built on half-truths? Could she trust the faint heartbeat of her blood that connected her to this shadowy world?

In the corner of the room, a dusty, leather-bound journal lay untouched. Emma hesitated before flipping it open, the scent of old paper filling her senses. As she traced her fingers over faded handwriting, a name jumped out—Francois, a figure she'd seen in her grandmother's photos, a man with sharp eyes and a reputation for whispers of underground dealings. Pages revealed coded messages, dates, and cryptic references to operations that spanned continents and decades. Emma's pulse quickened. This wasn't just about art or treasure. It was about a legacy of betrayal that had shaped her entire family—her grandmother's true story buried beneath layers of lies and silence. Somewhere within the faded ink was a truth that could change everything, if only she could decipher it.

The weight of her discovery pressed down harder when Emma found a hidden compartment within the journal, concealed behind a false lining. Inside, a small, torn photograph revealed a woman resembling her grandmother but with a different face—one younger, fierce, unrecognizable in her elegant portrait. Alongside it, a brittle letter addressed to 'Emma' in hurried handwriting. Every word hinted at a past she hadn't known, promising answers buried deep within the Montmartre apartment. The letter referenced a "key" and a "vault," yet spoke of danger looming if her search was not cautious. Emma's hands shook as she realized her pursuit of the truth wasn't just about uncovering family secrets—it could unveil a dangerous empire that had thrived in shadows for generations.

Outside the flickering candlelight, the city of Paris whispered of secrets. The narrow streets, cobbled with history and shadows, seemed to pulse with the rhythm of her ancestors' clandestine lives. Emma imagined her grandmother, young and fearless, darting through alleyways or slipping into hidden passages beneath Montmartre to evade capture. The more Emma uncovered, the clearer it became that the very ground she now stood on was a labyrinth of her family's past—an intricate network of passages, concealed doorways, and secret rooms built to hide more than just stolen art. Her mind raced with possibilities. What if the apartment itself was a vault? A fortress guarding secrets that could topple powerful figures and expose generations of treachery? She felt the thrill of discovery and the cold sting of danger, knowing that every step she took drew her closer to the heart of her heritage—and closer to those who would kill to keep it hidden.

Her focus sharpened as she recalled her grandmother's words: "The truth is buried beneath layers of time, waiting for someone brave enough to unearth it."

Emma's resolve hardened. With trembling hands, she packed several documents into her bag, knowing she had to move quickly. Shadows flitted across the room as she searched for the entry points her grandmother had described. The apartment's quiet seemed to pulse with anticipation. Somewhere nearby, a faint creak echoed—perhaps an old floorboard or something more sinister. Emma's pulse thrummed louder. She clenched her fists, ready to face whatever lay ahead. Somehow, she sensed the final pieces were within reach, and with them, the entire story of her family's hidden ties, tangled in lies and blood, waiting to be revealed at last.

8
The Montmartre Fortress

The faint glow of a flickering candle illuminated the narrow tunnel beneath Montmartre, casting dancing shadows on uneven stone walls. Emma's breath hitched as she and Liam crept forward, their footsteps muffled by decades of dust and silence. Every creak echoed like a secret screaming to be heard, the weight of history pressing down on them. The air was thick, a mixture of old brick, faded perfume, and something darker—unspoken dangers lurking just beyond sight. Their flashlights flickered uncertainly, illuminating a maze of corridors that seemed to breathe with the building's ancient heartbeat.

Emma paused at a fork in the passage, her fingers trembling as she traced faint carvings on the wall—symbols her grandmother had shown her in faded photographs. She pressed her palm against the rough surface, feeling the faint outline of a door hidden behind layers of plaster.

Liam studied the markings, eyes narrowing with curiosity.

"This looks like a map," he murmured, voice hushed but urgent.

The realization that these tunnels weren't just storage but deliberate, secret routes sent a shiver down Emma's spine. She knew these passages were vital, a skeletal network built during wartime, hiding more than just relics—they concealed truths that could change everything.

As Emma gently pushed against the concealed door, it shifted with a reluctant grind, revealing a dark gap beneath. Inside, the space was colder, the air thick with the scent of dampness and memories long buried. Flickering shadows revealed glimpse after glimpse of artifacts stacked in haphazard piles—stolen paintings, dusty documents, and rusted metallic objects that shimmered with promise and peril. Emma's heart pounded as she brushed her fingers across a torn cloth bearing the faded monogram of her grandmother's resistance group. There was a silent energy here, an unspoken Pact that had endured decades. Liam's eyes darted around, taking in the labyrinth of hidden chambers, each whispering stories of betrayal, courage, and concealment.

Suddenly, a loud click echoed behind them—faint but unmistakable. Emma spun around, her pulse quickening. Liam's face hardened as he pulled out his phone, only to find the screen darkening as if swallowed by an invisible force.

"They've hacked us," he whispered, voice taut with disbelief and fear. "Our phones—they're monitors now. Everything—every message, every move—you name it, it's being watched."

Emma's hands clenched into fists, frustration boiling inside her. Every step toward the truth brought them closer to danger, and now they knew that Margot's web stretched far beyond ancient art and secret passages. The very walls seemed to close in, whispering warnings of treachery, reminding them that someone—something—was determined to keep this buried at all costs.

In that moment, Emma's gaze fixed on a battered leather satchel tucked behind a loose stone. She reached out, her fingers trembling as she pulled it free. Inside, she discovered a bundle of aged papers, photographs, and a small, ornate box. The papers bore her grandmother's handwriting—records of transactions, names, dates—all meticulous, coded, and revealing a history darker than Emma had ever imagined. The photographs showed stolen artworks and signatures of powerful figures—corrupt officials, art dealers, and criminals intertwined in a decades-long conspiracy. Liam's eyes widened as he stared at the evidence, understanding flickering in his gaze. Beneath the surface of these humble tunnels lay a story of greed, deception, and family secrets that threatened to topple entire networks of stolen art and corruption.

Then, a sudden movement outside the chamber startled them. Shadows flickered at the edge of their vision—figures slipping silently into the passage. Emma's heart lurched as she saw a glint of metal—an armed figure creeping closer. Liam cursed softly, instinctively pulling Emma behind him as the door shuttered shut behind their intruders. In that suffocating silence, Emma realized with a sinking feeling—they had uncovered too much. Someone knew they were there, and it was only a matter of time before the walls closed in completely. The tunnel beneath Montmartre was more than a refuge—it was a trap, ready to enclose those brave enough to seek the truth. Emma clenched her fists, knowing that what they had found could either vindicate or destroy everything they fought for. Their fight had only just begun, and the shadows stretching ahead promised that danger lurked deeper than they had ever feared.

***

In the dim light filtering through the narrow, winding streets of Montmartre, Emma and Liam crouched behind a haphazard stack of crates in the shadowed alleyway. Their breaths came in ragged whispers, the weight of discovery pressing heavily on their shoulders. Every faint footstep or distant shout sent a jolt through their nerves, reminding them how thin the line was between safety and catastrophe. Emma's mind raced through her knowledge of art security, while Liam's eyes flicked over their surroundings, cataloging every possible escape route. They knew Margot's fortress—the hidden passages, the secret rooms—were within reach, but every moment they lingered, the danger grew closer to closing the final chapter of their plan.

She pulled out a battered notebook, crumpled from

months of scribbles, and flipped to the sketches she had made during their journey. The drawings of Montmartre's underground tunnels, the location of the secret chambers, and the obscure trapdoors were all contained within her notes. Liam studied her, catching the determination in her eyes, yet shadowed by a flicker of doubt. They'd come too far to let Margot slip away now. His mind sifted through the limited intel they'd managed to gather—an overheard conversation, a distinctive voice on a recording, the chilling recognition of her grandmother's name. Their goal was clear: get inside those hidden chambers, uncover the records, then shut down Margot's operation once and for all. But they both knew that to succeed, they'd need more than just courage—they'd need a flawless plan, ironclad and adaptable.

As they silently communicated with gestures, Emma unwrapped a small device Liam had fashioned from scraps he found in his bag—an improvised listening gadget, small enough to slip past any security measures Margot might have installed. The plan was simple yet dangerous: Liam would create a diversion, drawing operatives away from the main entrance while Emma slipped into the secret passages.

She had memorized the layout from her sketches, but navigating Margot's labyrinth required more than just memory—it required intuition and calmness under pressure. Outside, the faint hum of Montmartre's night life was replaced by an ominous silence, broken only by occasional distant footsteps or the faint clink of a broken window shutter. Time was running out, and every second she hesitated was a second closer to catastrophe.

Suddenly, a faint voice echoed from the alley's shadows, and both froze. Emma's heart pounded fiercely as Liam nodded and prepared to move. She adjusted her coat, clutching her small toolkit—a combination of lock-picking tools, tiny flashlights, and essential documents passed from Liam earlier. With a deep breath, she slipped around the corner, her footsteps muffled by the damp cobblestones, heading toward the first trapdoor her sketches indicated. Inside, the air was thick with dust and secrets, the faint glow of her flashlight illuminating age-old cobwebs that clung to the cracked stone walls. She moved cautiously, every creak sounding like a gunshot in her ears, knowing that Margot's loyal guards—or worse—could be lurking just beyond sight. Her palms were sweaty, but her resolve steadied her. This was the moment Margot's carefully guarded secrets would finally be uncovered.

Meanwhile, Liam, hidden in a side alley, kept a watchful eye on their surroundings. He muttered a prayer, running a hand through his hair as he typed rapid instructions into a tiny recording device, all while listening to the distant murmur of voices.

Their plan was unfolding, but the stakes had escalated—this wasn't just about stolen art anymore. It was about dismantling an empire, exposing the darkness that had thrived beneath Montmartre's picturesque façade for decades. As Emma's footsteps disappeared into the underground, Liam's grip tightened on his makeshift gadget, knowing that each second could be their last if Margot caught wind of their intentions. A gust of wind swept through, causing a loose sign above an old café to rattle, a reminder that nature and human treachery moved in tandem. All around them, the city seemed to hold its breath, waiting for the next move, the next secret to be revealed in the shadows.

***

The air beneath Montmartre hung thick with dust and the weight of secrets long buried. Emma moved cautiously through the labyrinthine corridors, her footsteps muffled on uneven stone. The faint flicker of her flashlight revealed glimpses of old brickwork—walls that seemed to breathe stories of betrayal and betrayal's aftermath. Every step felt like crossing into ghostly territory, where history had been hiding in shadows, waiting to be uncovered. She clutched her notebook tightly, senses heightened, knowing that the weight of what she might find could change everything.

Liam followed, his gaze darting from side to side, alert as a prey sensing danger. His hand brushed instinctively against the pistol tucked inside his coat—just in case there was more than secret passages and faded memories down here. He knew these tunnels weren't just relics; they were veins of a living criminal empire. Emma's discovery of the hidden rooms was no coincidence. Somewhere in these twisting corridors lay the proof they needed—evidence that would blow the lid off decades of lies and lies layered upon lies. Their breaths echoed softly in the silence, voices hushed but their hearts pounding with anticipation.

Near the end of the corridor, Emma's trembling fingers traced the rough surface of a stone wall. She pressed against it, and the wall moved slightly, revealing a narrow opening—an entrance to a secret chamber. Inside, the air grew colder, thick with the scent of stale air and history. Shelves lined the walls, piled high with yellowed papers, faded photographs, and fragile binders filled with handwritten records. Emma's eyes widened as she recognized the handwriting—her grandmother's. Every line, every note was a piece of a puzzle decades in the making. Somewhere in this room was proof of her family's darkest deeds, hidden beneath layers of dust and deception.

Liam stepped closer, scanning the records, his mind racing to connect dots long disjoint. The evidence was here. Pages filled with lists of stolen art, coded transactions, and names linked to a shadowy network operating through Europe. But what unnerved him more was a series of photographs pinned to the wall—images of people, some familiar, others strangers, all involved in the elaborate web of art theft. On the back of one picture, a date was scrawled in hurried ink—the day her grandmother disappeared. Emma's fingers trembled as she clutched the photo, realizing that her hunt for truth had led her deep into a dark underworld she had never truly understood. Every secret was inscribed here, waiting to rewrite her understanding of her own past.

Suddenly, Liam's phone buzzed violently in his pocket. Before he could silence it, a cold shiver ran down his spine—the screen lit up with a string of unfamiliar messages, encrypted and malicious. His face paled as he read the words:

"We know you're here. Stop digging or you'll regret it."

Emma noticed his expression and spun around, eyes narrowing. Their time was running out. Whoever was behind this knew their intentions, and the stakes had never been higher. As Liam discreetly pocketed the phone, Emma whispered:

"They've been watching us all along. We're not just

uncovering history—we're exposing a living nightmare."

A heavy silence settled as they realized they had crossed a line, into a place where trust was dangerous and secrets cost dearly. With their discovery secured in the dim light of the hidden chamber, they prepared to face what might come next—a confrontation that could shatter everything they believed, and might even cost them their lives.

9
Fighting for Justice

The air beneath the crowded attic was thick with silence, tension reverberating as Emma's heart pounded. Shadows danced along the cracked stone walls of the hidden chamber, remnants of centuries whispering secrets they weren't meant to tell. Margot stood at the center, her eyes cold and vacant, yet beneath that mask lay dangerous intent that betrayed her carefully crafted facade. Emma's fingers curled around the edge of a battered suitcase filled with records and photographs—her grandmother's clandestine stash—and every second felt like the fragile heartbeat of a secret waiting to explode. The stale air carried a faint metallic scent, mingling with dust and the faint whisper of footsteps outside, closing in. Emma knew this moment had been coming; each step, each revelation, had led them to this sharp edge, where truth and treachery collided in a final burst of clarity.

Liam, silent but tense, pressed close to Emma as he surveyed the narrow passageway behind Margot. Steel in his eyes, he moved slightly, positioning himself to block any sudden escape. Their temporary hideout beneath Montmartre had been minutes—feels like seconds—since they uncovered the last clue, a secret door concealed behind a false wall. Their pursuit of justice, once a distant hope, was now grinding toward a harsh, unavoidable showdown. Every bead of sweat on Liam's brow reminded him of the stakes—this was no longer about secrets buried for decades; it was about the lives at risk, about stopping a criminal empire that had thrived on betrayal and blood. Emma's breath caught as Margot's lips curled into a thin smile, one that signified a storm was about to break loose. Emma tightened her grip on the records, knowing these documents held the power to tear down everything Margot had built.

Margot finally stepped forward, her heels clicking sharply on the uneven floor. Her voice, calm yet sinister, cut through the tense air like a flickering blade.

"You really think you've won? After all these years, you believe you can walk away from what's already done? This is just the beginning."

Her eyes flicked to the window, where faint light filtered in, casting ominous shadows. Emma's mind raced, every memory flashing—the stolen art, the betrayals, the countless lies spun to hide her true purpose. Margot's smile widened as she produced a small, ornate pistol from her coat pocket, fingers tightening around the grip. The room seemed to shrink, the silence stretching like a tight wire ready to snap.

Emma's pulse hammered in her ears. Liam's hand moved instinctively, reaching for her side, knowing this was the moment that would forever define their fight—justice teetering on the edge of chaos.

The door suddenly burst open — not by Margot's hand, but by the sudden crashing of footsteps. Several figures appeared, masked and furious, faces obscured in the dim light but their presence undeniable.

The realization hit like a punch—these weren't just petty thieves or simple accomplices; they were part of Margot's network—dangerous, well-armed, and determined to protect her at any cost. Emma's eyes darted to Liam, who instinctively pulled out his phone. No signal. Their devices had been compromised—clones, just as they feared. Outside, the distant sound of sirens echoed, distant but growing louder, a reminder that the outside world was closing in. Margot's voice snapped through the chaos, bitter and triumphant.

"You think you can stop what's already in motion? The art is mine, and there's no way out now."

As the room filled with shouts and the glint of

weapons, Emma knew that their fight was reaching its zenith, one final battle that would determine the future of everything they'd come to believe in.

In that heated moment, Liam and Emma made eye contact. The silent pledge passing between them was more powerful than words—survival, truth, justice. They ducked behind a heavy wooden table as shots rang out, dust swirling around like gray fog.

Margot lunged forward, her pistol aimed but nervous, her hand trembling just slightly. Emma moved swiftly, her mind racing to piece together her grandmother's records, the clues that might save them all. She knew Margot's empire was built on layers of deception, layered deep beneath Montmartre's streets, in tunnels and rooms designed long ago for hideouts and secrets. Explosions of sound erupted outside—the clash between their resolve and the astounding betrayal they had uncovered. It was as if the very ground beneath their feet was shattering, and Emma, trembling but resolved, prepared herself for the last act—the moment when everything would hang in the balance, with countless lives depending on their courage.

***

The room was a flurry of hurried movements and flickering screens as Liam adjusted his camera, the live feed now humming through the digital ether. Every second felt charged, the weight of their discovery pressing down on them like storm clouds ready to burst. Emma sat beside him, her breath shallow, eyes glued to the monitor displaying the first fragments of their evidence.

This was the moment they had fought for, yet the danger lurking behind the scenes was more imminent than ever. They had come too far to falter now—a single broadcast could unravel Margot's empire, or cement their downfall. The apartment beneath Montmartre's winding streets was silent save for the faint hum of the equipment. Emma's hands trembled slightly as she double-checked the camera angles and sound feeds.

The shadows that danced across the room seemed to whisper secrets, memories of Margot's long history woven into the very walls. Liam kept glancing at Emma, sensing her resolve, but also her nerves. Behind her calm exterior, he knew she was still haunted by the past—by everything at stake. They had a narrow window now, and every moment counted. This wasn't just about exposing crime; it was about justice, truth in the face of a family's dark legacy.

Jammed into the corner was a makeshift control panel—the small hub of their operation—where Liam was orchestrating the live broadcast. His finger hovered over the button that would send their evidence into the world. The feed was encrypted, carefully set to auto-stream to trusted contacts and media channels they coordinated with just in case. The plan was simple on paper: reveal the hidden records, expose Margot's crimes, and let the world see her for what she truly was. But simple plans rarely survive first contact with reality. Shadows slipped at their periphery, and the distant tremor of footsteps suggested they weren't alone in this fight. Emma's heart pounded. No turning back now.

As Liam prepared to activate the broadcast, a faint

noise interrupted the tense silence—a soft click from the hallway outside. Emma froze. Her eyes widened in alarm. Someone was trying to enter. Liam instinctively reached for his phone, but it was dead—hacked, like everything else. The digital fortress was no longer secure. Outside, the shadows moved with purpose, silent but deliberate. The walls beneath Montmartre had witnessed secrets for centuries, and now they echoed with the footfalls of enemies closing in. Emma's pulse quickened as she realized this wasn't just a technical glitch or a failed signal—it was a breach. Someone had found them, or worse, was about to cut off their lifeline from revealing the truth that could topple a empire.

***

The city outside Paris blurred past in a hurried shadow, but inside the battered car, every breath felt like a reminder of the danger closing in. Emma stared at the rearview mirror, her hands trembling on the wheel, trying to ignore the tightening knot in her stomach. She had thought they were finally free, that the nightmare would end once they reached the outskirts of the city. Yet, her instincts told her something was wrong—the quiet stretching too long, the too-perfect silence of their tail. Shadows flickered at her periphery, or so her mind imagined, fueling a restless paranoia she'd learned to hide.

Liam sat silently beside her, eyes fixed on the dim streetlights flickering past. His jaw was clenched, muscles tight with the weight of recent discoveries—that Margot might not just be the orchestrator of art thefts, but the mastermind behind a broader web of deception. The call from his handler had come moments before, a terse message that confirmed their worst fears: Margot had set a trap, and she had eyes everywhere. The false sense of safety that had accompanied their escape now crumbled into a haunting realization that every step they took might be a step into her carefully laid trap.

They reached a narrow, shadowed alley—they thought it was their moment to breathe, to disappear into the Parisian night. But as Liam looked out the window, a figure stepped into the glow of a broken streetlamp. It was small, quick, and moved with purpose. Emma's heart pounded so fiercely she feared it might burst from her chest. The figure's hand shot out, signaling silently, flags fluttering like distant echoes of a war neither of them fully understood. Liam reached for his phone, but the screen blinked to life—cloned, hacked, useless. Every communication, every plan, was now in Margot's control.

Before they could react, the car's door handle rattled, then paused. An ominous silence fell over the vehicle—a moment frozen in a frenzied rush of thoughts. Emma realized with a sinking dread that the apartment in Montmartre, once seemingly a safe haven, might have been compromised from the start. Every detail, every clue they had uncovered, now felt hollow. Margot's plan was unfolding with cruel precision, echoing through the streets in whispers only they could hear. The chase wasn't over; it was merely entering its darkest, most dangerous phase.

Suddenly, Liam's phone buzzed violently in his pocket. The screen flashed a number he didn't recognize, but the caller ID sent a shiver through him—Deep State. A split-second decision, then he answered. The voice on the line was cold, distant, and unmistakable—the unmistakable tone of betrayal.

"Your investigation is compromised," it said, flatly. "Your movements are monitored. Margot is not just a thief. She's the puppet master, and she's been pulling every string for decades."

Emma's eyes widened as the weight of it all sank in. This wasn't just about stolen art. It was about a legacy of deception that threatened to rewrite history, and now, they were running out of time to stop it.

The car's engine roared to life as Liam snapped the phone shut. The small figure outside disappeared into the shadows, leaving behind a trail of unanswered questions. Emma's mind raced, her thoughts colliding like fragments of a shattered mirror—fissures of truth, lies, and betrayals that blurred in the darkness. Margot's twisted empire was more than she had imagined, deeply rooted beneath the cobbled streets of Montmartre, hidden behind walls of secrets. Every step forward drew them closer to the truth, but also closer to danger. And as the city of lights cast its faint glow, Emma knew this was no longer a game of shadows—it was a fight for every piece of her soul, every fragment of her family's history, and perhaps, the very legacy that Margot had spent her life meticulously hiding beneath the mask of a grandmother.

10
The Truth Revealed

The narrow beam of the flashlight flickered against the rough stone walls, casting long shadows that danced with each step Emma took deeper into the hidden chamber. Her fingers traced the cold surfaces of the countless boxes and binders stacked in haphazard rows, as if her own curiosity was trying to peel back layers of concealed history. These records, dusty and forgotten, held the weight of decades—perhaps even more, whispering secrets only silence and time could keep. Emma's heart pounded in her chest not just from the rush of discovery but from the realization that they might finally unlock the truth her grandmother had shielded her from all her life. Somewhere in this chaos of paper and ink lay the key to everything—truths about stolen art, betrayals buried beneath layers of deception, and a legacy she never knew she carried.

Every ledger she opened was a story carved into faded ink. Files documented transactions, names, dates, and clandestine deals, some marked with symbols known only to those who understood the language of art crime. Dust billowed into the air as she carefully sifted through a binder labeled in faded handwriting:

Operations—Montmartre 1942

Her breath hitched. These pages weren't just records; they were a map of her grandmother's life—her clandestine role in the Resistance, her involvement in hiding stolen masterpieces, and most troubling of all, her connection to a sprawling network of thieves that stretched far beyond what Emma ever feared.

As she flipped through the pages, a photograph slipped out—a black-and-white snapshot of Margot Dubois, younger, eyes sharp and defiant, standing amid a group of men with concealed faces. Emma clutched it tightly, trembling as the weight of her discovery pressed down upon her.

Meanwhile, Liam waited outside the chamber, his eyes darting anxiously between the narrow corridor and the doorway. The faint hum of distant voices echoed from the main hall of what they'd thought was an abandoned building—until now. His mind raced with the implications. These records weren't just relics; they were the skeletons of an empire built on greed, lies, and betrayal. Margot's secret life was a web that entangled the highest echelons of society, shielding her from justice for over seventy years. And Emma, unearthing this hidden archive, had become a direct threat. Liam knew they didn't have much time before someone came to silence them forever. The hairs on his arms bristled as he played the moment in his mind's eye, feeling the pulse of danger creeping closer, waiting for the inevitable.

Within the confines of that underground vault, another discovery made Emma pause—another package wrapped carefully in oilcloth, sealed with aged wax. Inside, she found a bundle of letters—dozens, yellowed and fragile—covering a range of years, revealing clandestine exchanges between her grandmother and unknown figures. As she held one in trembling hands, her eyes widened. The handwriting was delicate yet urgent, describing meetings, deals, and a series of coded references to a "treasure" hidden in Montmartre. Every line sent shivers down her spine. These letters painted a picture of Margot not as a victim but as a master manipulator—someone who had spent her life orchestrating a masterstroke of deception. Emma's fingers curled into fists, realizing that her pursuit of her grandmother's secrets was dirtier than she had imagined—an intricate game with stakes high enough to destroy everything she believed in.

****

Weeks after Emma uncovered the secrets buried beneath her grandmother's fragile veneer, the truth about the famed Monet paintings began to surface, but not in the way she had anticipated. Hidden within the records Margot had meticulously kept were details of an intricate web of deception, forged signatures, and stolen masterpieces that spanned decades. Emma's fingers trembled as she sifted through faded papers, each page revealing a chapter of chaos that her family desperately tried to bury. The more she discovered, the clearer it became that her lineage was not merely about art but about a clandestine society of con artists, thieves, and traitors hiding behind a crown of artistic brilliance. Now, looking at the collection of genuine documents, Emma realized that real value was in these stories—tales of betrayal, love, loss, and survival—etched into fragile paper, waiting to be told.

Among the dusty records, Emma found a battered ledger filled with handwritten notes—names, dates, and stolen invoices, all referencing artworks by Monet, but with aliases, coded symbols, and cryptic comments. Each entry was a puzzle piece, hinting at a much larger operation. Her heart pounded at the thought that the treasure her grandmother spoke of wasn't a simple thing to hold or possess, but a tale woven into the very fabric of her family's dark history. It was as if each stroke of her pen unlocked a chapter in the twisted chronicle of the infamous Monet forgeries that had kept her enthralled for years. She could feel the presence of Margot lurking in every shadow, the echoes of her manipulative whispers filling the silent attic as Emma grappled with the American-born artist's legacy—one fraught with deception, hope, and regret. It was a legacy that now beckoned Emma to confront secrets buried deep in her bloodline, secrets that threatened to undo everything she thought she knew about her heritage.

The walls of the Montmartre apartment, dimly lit by the flickering glow of a single bulb, seemed alive with the weight of hidden truths. Emma's fingers traced the worn wood of a secret door she'd discovered behind a false panel. It revealed a narrow passage—an escape route her grandmother had crafted long ago, designed to hide her most precious secrets from prying eyes. As Emma peered into the darkness, a cold shiver ran down her spine. Was Margot still watching? Had her grandmother left behind more than just records? Every creak of the old building seemed amplified, echoing the fragile line between safety and danger. Emma's mind raced: moments ago, she had uncovered enough evidence to cripple her grandmother's empire forever, yet the shadows in the room whispered warnings of retaliation. Outside the window, a faint flicker of movement caught her eye—a figure slipping through the alley, unseen but undeniable.

Emma realized then that her quest for the truth had awakened something far more sinister. The monster lurking in her family's history was stirring once again, and her time to confront it was running out.

In the trembling quiet, Liam suddenly appeared

beside her, his face a mask of intensity.

"Emma," he whispered, voice low, "I think they're onto us."

His eyes darted toward the door, then back at her with a mixture of alarm and determination. The air between them grew thick with unspoken fears, each of them aware that their pursuit of justice might have crossed an invisible line. Liam unzipped his jacket, revealing a small USB drive—an insurance policy, he said, stored with the evidence they'd collected. Their collars were hot with the pressure of imminent danger. The key question hovered in the heavy silence: could they trust anyone anymore? Every face in their journey—every stranger, every friendly face at the station—could be a threat. Liam's voice broke the tense spell:

"We've got one chance. If we don't move now, they're going to silence us for good."

Emma clenched her fists, her mind racing through plans and escape routes, knowing that in the shadows of Montmartre, the ghost of her grandmother's past was watching, waiting for her next move. The night was closing in, and so was the threat that could dismantle any hope they had left. Somewhere out there,

Margot's web grew tighter, and the game was about to reach its deadly climax.

***

Emma sat silently in the dimly lit room, the faint glow of city lights filtering through the cracked shutters. She traced her finger along the edge of the battered leather-bound ledger she'd found tucked away behind a false wall in Margot's hidden library beneath Montmartre. Each page was a window into decades of secrets—records of stolen art, clandestine transactions, and names long believed lost to history. The weight of the truth pressed heavily on her chest, promising to unravel not only her grandmother's tangled past but also a web that ensnared countless innocent families, their stories buried in silence for too long.

The air was thick with anticipation. Liam watched her with a mixture of awe and concern as she carefully flipped through the aged pages, noting the meticulous handwriting and faded stamp marks. Somewhere in this room lay the key to justice—a missing piece of the past that could finally silence the ghosts haunting their present. Every second felt like a fragile thread holding together the fragile fabric of their fragile hope. Outside, the city hummed unaware of the storm of revelations brewing beneath their feet, a storm that threatened to sweep away lies built over generations.

As Emma uncovered a sealed envelope marked with her grandmother's initials, her heart pounded with a mix of fear and resolve. The handwriting was hurried, almost desperate—an urgent warning or perhaps a final plea. Carefully, she slid the fragile paper from its hiding place, realizing it contained not just words but a series of cryptic coordinates and a single phrase: "The true treasure lies in what's unseen."

Liam leaned in, eyes narrowing as he considered the implications. Whatever was concealed here wasn't merely a stash of stolen artworks; it was something far more potent, something capable of toppling an empire built on deception and bloodshed.

Suddenly, the distant hum of footsteps echoed

above their heads, briefly startling them into tense silence. Emma's fingers froze on the edge of the letter. She sensed movement, a presence lurking just beyond the walls, watching. Her mind raced—could Margot have had eyes on them all along? Had she known someone was digging through her secrets? The room felt colder, shadows stretching longer as a strange chill crept down her spine. Every glance over her shoulder felt like a warning that they were running out of time—an ominous countdown ticking faster with each passing second.

Then the faint click of a door latch broke the silence. Emma's breath hitched as she instinctively pressed her hand against Liam's arm, her mind scrambling for a plan. Their discovery was dangerous enough, but now they knew someone else was aware of their intrusion. Was it Margot herself, securing her treasure trove before the last pieces fell into place? Or a follower, a shadow of the past come to life? The room's stillness became deafening, every heartbeat hammering in her ears as they prepared for what might come next—uncertain whether the next movement would save them or condemn them to the depths of Margot's forgotten past.

II
Aftermath and Justice

The moment the police burst into the cramped apartment in Montmartre, Emma felt her heart threaten to break free from her chest. The walls, once echoing with whispered secrets and hidden passages, now reverberated with the cacophony of shouts and shuffling feet. Margot's figure emerged from the shadows, her eyes cold and calculating, as if she had anticipated this moment long ago. Emma's hands clenched the edge of a dusty table, her mind racing to comprehend the gravity of what was unfolding. The air thickened with tension—not just from the arrests happening around her, but from the realization that their entire quest might be about to crash down in pieces.

Officers moved swiftly, their flashlights piercing the darkness, illuminating stacks of stolen artworks, forged documents, and meticulously kept records. Margot's crisp voice tried to maintain composure as she was handcuffed, but beneath the veneer of calm was a flicker of defiance. Emma watched as her grandmother's face flickered with a strange mix of regret and pride—perhaps for the life of deception she had built, or for the daughter she had unknowingly endangered. The weight of truth pressed down on Emma, heavy as the stone floors beneath her. She had fought so hard to uncover this labyrinthine web, only to see it unravel in her hands, her heart pounding with a mixture of victory and loss.

The police led Margot away, her heels clicking ominously on the cobblestone street, echoing like a countdown. Emma and Liam stood at the threshold of their victory, yet the silence that followed felt unnatural, ominous. Liam's eyes searched her face, the flicker of relief tempered by a disturbing revelation. Emma's mind churned with questions—had Margot been acting alone? Was this truly the end, or just a temporary pause before something darker emerged from the shadows? As the distant sirens faded into the night, Emma knew the consequences of this arrest would ripple across her life, her family's legacy, and the intricate web of secrets she'd just begun to piece together.

News of Margot's detention spread like wildfire. Journalists swarmed the scene, eager to capture the villain's fall, but Emma held back, her thoughts a storm of turmoil. The truth was far messier than any headline. Margot's empire was built on decades of lies, art stolen from the dead, and alliances shadowed by betrayal. The controversy surrounding her arrest stirred debates everywhere—how much of her crimes were driven by desperation, and how much by pure greed? Emma's phone buzzed endlessly, messages flooding her inbox from allies, skeptics, and old friends turning their backs. The personal stakes had blurred into a relentless quest for justice, leaving her exhausted but determined to see it through.

In the days that followed, Emma was thrust into a whirlwind of investigations, legal battles, and media scrutiny. Her role in the case became clearer—she wasn't just an investigator now, but a symbol of resilience amid darkness. Yet beneath the surface, she grappled with a profound sense of loss. Margot, her own flesh and blood, was responsible for crimes that tainted her family's history. Emotions clashed—anger, grief, and a strange flicker of understanding, even sympathy. Emma knew that her future depended on unraveling the tangled threads of this web, discovering whether Margot's arrest was a beginning or merely a pause. One thing was certain: the shadow of Margot's legacy would linger long after the verdict was handed down, defining Emma's journey in ways she had never imagined possible.

Liam, meanwhile, found himself caught between relief and suspicion. The truth about Margot's empire was only part of the story; shadows still lurked in the corners of this conspiracy. His undercover work had led him here, but the aftermath was another battlefield. As he watched Emma navigate the storm, he realized their lives had become irrevocably intertwined. The trust they had built during their perilous days beneath Montmartre's streets was now tested by betrayal and hidden motives. Liam pondered whether he had uncovered the whole truth or if something even darker remained concealed beneath the surface. The consequences of Margot's arrest would ripple across international borders—her influence reaching into the highest echelons of power, her bonds to corrupt officials and black markets still unbroken. The effort to dismantle her network would stretch far beyond these dark corridors, and Emma and Liam knew that this victory was only the start.

As Margot sat silently in her holding cell, her gaze distant and unreadable, a quiet smile touched her lips—an expression that felt almost like a farewell. She understood that her reign was ending but believed her legacy would endure, reborn from the chaos she had ignited. Emma's resolve hardened; the path ahead was still fraught with danger. The arrest cracked open a door to a trove of secrets that would soon surface, revealing not just Margot's deeds but the entire machinery behind her crimes. Emma clung to the hope that justice was within reach, even as the shadows threatened to swallow everything she held dear. Deep below the surface of her victory, a whisper warned her that this was merely the first act in a much larger story—one that would test her limits and challenge her notions of family, loyalty, and truth. In the storm of chaos, Emma found her resolve sharper than ever, ready to face whatever consequences awaited beyond the walls of her grandmother's fallen empire.

***

The narrow streets of Montmartre had always felt like a maze, winding around secrets and stories long hidden. Now, beneath its cobblestones and quaint cafés, Emma and Liam uncovered a labyrinth of secrets—that of Margot Dubois's clandestine world. They found a hidden staircase tucked behind a false wall in the apartment, leading down to secret tunnels that seemed to breathe history and danger alike. Dust particles floated in the dim light as they stepped cautiously into the darkness, each step echoing the weight of decades of lies. Walls lined with faded photographs and crumbling documents told silent stories of art thefts, double-crosses, and a life lived in shadows.

Emma's fingers trembled as she traced over a concealed latch, revealing a hidden passageway that wove beneath the entire building. The air grew cooler and thicker with silence, punctuated only by the distant drip of water echoing through the tunnels. They moved quietly, knowing that discovery at this moment could mean losing everything—except, perhaps, their lives. Their flashlights flickered against graffiti and cryptic symbols scrawled by past occupants, marking routes only insiders understood. Every turn revealed another secret—an abandoned crate, a rusted bicycle, even a faint scent of smoke long extinguished, whispering of past clandestine meetings. The truth, buried deep within these tunnels, waited for them to unravel it.

As Emma held her breath, Liam carefully pushed aside a heavy curtain of cobwebs, exposing a concealed door lined with strange symbols. His heart pounded—this was no ordinary hiding spot. Inside, they uncovered stacks of faded records, faded enough to be barely readable yet still ominously revealing. Files documenting art deals, black-market transactions, and names of key players snaked across the pages, their ink faded but their secrets intact. Emma's eyes widened as realization struck—this was the heart of Margot's operation, a vault of her lifetime's work. Everything pointed to these secrets being the key to dismantling the entire criminal web. And somewhere within the darkness, the true danger lurked—waiting for the wrong move to reveal itself.

***

The narrow cobblestone streets of Montmartre seemed to swallow Emma and Liam whole as they hurried through its shadows. It was late, but the city never truly slept—its quiet corners hiding more than just stories. Every alley seemed to whisper secrets, and the distant hum of Paris's nightlife faded behind the urgent pounding of their hearts.

They moved with purpose, knowing Margot's ghost was closer than ever, watching from the darkness. Inside the old building, they found a battered wooden door loaded with strange symbols and a faint scent of old paper and secrets.

Emma pushed the door open slowly, the hinges protesting with a squeal that echoed in the hollow silence. Inside, hidden passages wound beneath the city, places where shadows formed walls and whispers clung to the air. Dust motes floated in streaks of moonlight that seeped through cracks between stones, illuminating moldered records and crates filled with stolen art. Emma's fingers brushed over a faded ledger—her grandmother's handwriting still visible, an intricate dance of dates, names, and transactions that stretched back decades. It was more than evidence; it was a relic of history's darkest chapters, waiting to tell their story.

Liam checked his phone—the flickering screen confirmed it; their signals were scrambled, their devices compromised. Every glance over their shoulders felt like a threat, as if invisible eyes observed every move. They spread out, each seeking clues; Emma's focus drifted to a corner where a secret door concealed a tiny room. Inside, a cache of photographs, handwritten notes, and coded documents confirmed her worst fears. Margot's empire wasn't just a collection of stolen art; it was a meticulously crafted network that spanned continents and decades. Every name, every transaction, was another thread pulling her deeper into a web of lies.

The air grew heavier as Emma's heartbeat quickened. Sweat beaded on her temples, and a shiver ran down her spine—this wasn't just a treasure hunt anymore. It was a war, and their adversary was eager to close every escape route. Suddenly, Liam's voice cut through the silence, urgent and low.

"We need to get out of here, now."

Emma nodded, gripping her bag tightly, feeling

the full weight of their discovery pressing against her chest. Behind them, the shadows seemed to shift, and she knew Margot's reach extended far and wide—this wasn't just about stolen art. It was about legacy, betrayal, and the darkness that cloaked her entire family line.

Footsteps echoed faintly above, muffled but persistent. Emma pressed her hand against the cool stone wall, feeling the rough texture of decades of secrets layered beneath her fingertips. Liam glanced at her and then at the narrow tunnel ahead, both understanding that they had uncovered enough to topple an empire. Yet, Margot was never a woman who left loose ends. The walls around them seemed to close in, promising that the confrontation they prepared for was only moments away. As they moved deeper into the labyrinth, a faint gleam from a hidden corner caught Emma's eye—a small box, wrapped in velvet, with a delicate latch.

Her breath hitched. The box was the key, or perhaps a trap. She hesitated briefly before slipping her hand inside, mind racing with what it could hold. Inside, she found a bundle of aged papers—photographs of stolen art, documents with signatures she didn't recognize, and a small, faded jewel that radiated a cold, unsettling energy. She realized this was the heart of her grandmother's secret—proof of a legacy built on deception, blood, and silence. Liam watched her carefully, understanding that this discovery was no ordinary find; it was a revelation that could change everything. Both of them, tangled in a story darker than they'd imagined, now stood on the precipice of exposure—knowing full well that Margot, their ruthless matriarch, lurked just beyond sight, waiting for the moment to strike back.

12
Love and Reconnections

The train jerked suddenly, a seismic shudder that made everyone lurch forward. Emma clutched her notebook, the pages fluttering like captive birds, her heart pounding in her chest. She shot a quick glance at Liam, who sat beside her, eyes fixed on the dark window but ears suddenly alert. The storm outside was relentless, wind screaming like a banshee as rain battered the carriage in relentless sheets. No one had spoken much since the last delay, yet a weight had settled, thick and unspoken, hanging over them like a shadow cast in a moment of chaos.

The dim glow of the emergency overhead lights cast eerie shadows on Liam's face. His jaw was clenched tight, every muscle taut beneath his rugged features. Emma sensed he was holding more than just the storm—she could feel the tension threading through him, like invisible wires pulled too tight. Their initial conversations, tentative and cautious, had morphed into a shared silence filled with unspoken fears. Some-where in the distant, muffled thunder, Emma felt the whisper of memories—fragile truths pushing against the edges of her mind, threatening to spill over at any moment.

In the flickering light, Emma's gaze drifted to her sketches. Carefully detailed architectural diagrams, drawn late at night in her quiet studio, now seemed to pulse with a new urgency. They captured every angle of her surroundings—the camera placements, emergency exits, even the flickering security lights. She hadn't meant to unveil so much—drawing was supposed to quiet her nerves, a shield against the storm inside her. But Liam's sharp eyes caught the meticulous lines, and in them, Emma glimpsed a flicker of suspicion. Her fingers froze for a heartbeat, then quickly pushed the notebook closed. A sense of vulnerability hit her harder than the rolling thunder outside. What if he saw too much?

The train shuddered again, more violently this time, and Emma's stomach clenched. She caught Liam watching her, a flicker of curiosity—or was it suspicion?—crossing his face. Before she could say anything, the carriage door at the far end yawned open, a gust of wind swirling inside, carrying the scent of rain and something else—something darker. A shadow moved. Liam's tense posture stiffened, and Emma could see the moment his voice went from casual to alert.

"Did you hear that?" he whispered, voice low but firm.

Emma nodded, her pulse pounding louder. The storm was no longer just outside; it had infiltrated their fragile refuge, and with it, the shadows of secrets neither of them dared to fully face.

Late that night, under the pale light of a flickering lantern, Emma sat silently in the corner, her breathing shallow. Across from her, Liam paced like a predator caught in a trap, his expression unreadable. She saw him speak into his phone in hurried, clipped words—an unfamiliar language that made her skin crawl. His voice sounded urgent, almost desperate, whispering about "the package" and "the deadline," as if time itself had become a villain pressing down on them. Emma's mind raced—her grandmother's letter had spoken of a "treasure," of hidden truths buried deep within Montmartre. But what if the letter was more than a faded memory? What if she was walking into something dangerous, darker than she could have imagined?

For the first time, Emma questioned her instincts. Was her pursuit of the past leading her into a trap? Every shadow took on new meaning. Every creak, every muffled sound, seemed to whisper warnings. The train's delayed journey now felt less like a mere weather inconvenience; it was a deliberate act—an orchestrated pause, a tense standoff where everything was at stake. Emma watched Liam, whose jaw was clenched tight, his eyes darting back and forth, alive with the secrets he'd been hiding. She wondered if she could trust him—or if, somehow, both of them had been pulled into something they didn't fully understand. Outside, the storm raged on, unyielding, relentless. Inside, a fragile alliance formed amid the chaos, a bond forged in the dark, waiting to either endure or shatter under pressure.

***

Emma sat silently in the cramped corner of the Montmartre apartment, her fingers trembling as she traced the edges of the faded photographs on the wall.

The room was thick with dust, yet every inch seemed to whisper secrets of a life long buried. Her mind spun with the possibilities: what discovery could truly change everything? She looked over at Liam, whose brow was lined with concentration, as if mapping out an escape plan he'd barely voiced aloud. For so long, they'd walked separate paths—her in shadows and whispers, him in a blur of danger and truth. Now, amid this chaos, the idea of their future blossomed, fragile but undeniable, like a fragile seed ready to break through concrete.

They had come through chaos, each battered and scarred, yet driven by a shared determination. Emma knew that this wasn't just about fighting back against Margot's empire; it was about what they could build once the dust settled. Tomorrow, they would stare at the horizon and decide whether love, forged in fire and forged anew in danger, could become something more solid—something worth fighting for in the days ahead. The thought stirred within her a cautious hope, a flicker of light she hadn't allowed herself in years. As Liam moved closer, their shoulders brushed, and he looked into her eyes with a seriousness that made her realize that the biggest step wasn't behind them, but yet to come.

There was a quiet rhythm to their planning, a hesitant dance of words and gestures that spoke of trust after so much betrayal. Emma traced the line of her grandmother's hidden records, planning how they would decode the labyrinth of secrets buried beneath Montmartre's streets. Liam pulled out the battered notebook he'd kept—maps, clues, scribbles of a story that was more than just art theft. They both knew that beyond the immediate danger lay a future shaped by choices they had yet to make. How could they possibly chart a life amid a maze of lies, stolen treasures, and ghostly memories? Yet, the desire to find a way, to turn the chaos into a new beginning, shimmered quietly like dawn's first light spilling through cracked panes.

In the stillness, Emma finally broke the silence, her voice soft but resolute.

"We have to decide what comes next. We can't let this be just a fleeting moment—something to forget when turmoil passes."

Liam nodded, the weight of their shared revelations pressing between them.

"The only future I see," he murmured, "is the one

we fight for, together. Whatever it takes. We build it on trust, on truth—on leaving behind this tangled past."

The words hung in the air like a fragile bridge, a promise of surrender to hope rather than despair. Their hands reached out then, tentative but firm—a beginning. In that small, battered room, amid remnants of stolen pasts, they dared to look ahead, imagining a world where love could survive amid ruins.

Stepping closer, Liam gently touched her hand, his eyes searching hers.

"We're not just planning to escape, he whispered. We're planning a future. One where the truths we uncover finally bring peace. I believe in that."

Emma squeezed his fingers, her heart pounding with a mixture of fear and hope. They couldn't predict what lay ahead, but in this moment—this fragile, trembling moment—they took the first real step toward reclaiming what had been lost. Night settled outside, but within, a new dawn beckoned. Dreaming of a life beyond the shadows, they began to sketch a future, uncertain but theirs alone to create. A future where love might bloom anew, forged in understanding and defiance—ready to face whatever storms would come next.

Outside, the city beneath their battered refuge continued its restless pulse, unaware of the lives about to transform beneath its ancient stones. Emma looked around, imagining the day they would walk away from these secrets, hand in hand, leaving behind their fears. Liam's gaze lingered on her, a resolute spark igniting in his eyes. Together, they would decide how to move forward, brick by brick, step by step. The past was a maze of shadows, but the future—nothing was certain yet—held promises they couldn't ignore. As dawn threatened to break through the cracked window, their unspoken vow whispered silently: no matter what they faced, they would face it united, building from the chaos a new life worth fighting for.

✳✳✳

Emma sat quietly in the dimly lit café near Montmartre, her eyes tracing the misty silhouettes of rooftops outside the stained glass. The weight of the past weeks pressed heavily on her shoulders, yet an odd sense of calm lingered within her. She thought about the perilous days they had survived, the secrets uncovered beneath the ancient streets, and the man who had become her anchor through it all. The chaos, once deafening, now softened into a distant hum beneath her thoughts, reminiscent of the storm that had halted their train in its tracks. Behind her, the clatter of cups and murmured conversations faded into a background hum, as if the city itself was holding its breath, waiting for her to breathe out her memories. Her fingers idly traced the edges of her battered journal, filled with sketches and notes—testaments to a journey that had turned her world upside down.

Looking back, she realized how each twist and turn had transformed her. There'd been moments when she'd thought hope was lost, when shadows of betrayal crept into every corner, tainting even her most cherished memories. The day she discovered her grandmother's real story had been like unraveling a delicate web, each strand pulling her further into questions she hadn't dared ask before. Her past as an investigator, once a distant part of her identity, had come roaring back with fierce clarity, forcing her to confront the demons she'd tried to bury. Liam's presence had shattered her defenses at just the right moment—his unexpected honesty and quiet strength mirroring her own resilience. She smiled softly, remembering how he'd looked at her with eyes that saw more than surface secrets—for the first time, she felt a flicker of hope glow within, like a fragile flame that refused to die out.

Their journey had been riddled with danger, lies, and betrayal. They'd uncovered Margot's labyrinth of crimes, hidden in secret chambers beneath Montmartre, where echoes of her past deeds reverberated through time. The paperwork, photographs, and maps they'd discovered ached with history, each piece a chapter in a story that threatened to swallow them whole. And yet, amid the chaos, their bond had grown—an unlikely alliance forged in fire and shared peril. Liam's steady presence had become a lifeline, a reminder that even in the darkest moments, human connection could shine through. Emma thought about the day they'd confronted Margot, the tense waiting in that hidden underground room, nerves taut as steel, breath held in anticipation. It had felt like stepping into history herself, each decision a gambit in a game that could end in ruin or redemption.

She brushed her hand over the delicate scar at her wrist—the one Liam had gently bandaged that night they'd escaped the crumbling apartment. It wasn't just a mark of injury; it was a symbol of trust, a reminder of everything they'd fought through. Turning her gaze to the crows circling above, she wondered how far she'd come from that scared, uncertain woman who'd boarded a train seeking refuge. Now she knew her strength had grown from the roots of her roots, from understanding her family's secrets and accepting her own. The detective in her whispered that this wasn't the end but merely the start of something new, something better. Liam's voice echoed softly in her memory, promising that their fight wasn't over—that they had unfinished business, and perhaps, new beginnings waiting beyond these shadowed streets. She took a deep breath, feeling the city's pulse drumming beneath her skin. Her journey had reshaped her, hemming her into a new version—scarred, yes, but unbroken.

In that quiet moment, Emma wondered if she'd truly reflected enough, if she'd given herself the grace to mourn her losses and celebrate her victories. She thought about the stolen art, the lives restored, the future unfolding in her mind. Most of all, she felt the flicker of hope for Liam, who had become more than a companion—he was her partner in every sense. She looked out at the swirling fog, a mirror to her own swirling thoughts, and realized something profound. The path ahead was uncertain, tangled with secrets yet to be uncovered, dangers lurking just beyond sight. But as long as they faced it together, nothing could truly break them. Their hearts—tested by fire—now beat in unison, resilient and ready. In that moment of quiet reflection, Emma knew that from the wreckage of her past, a new story was taking shape—one of love, strength, and the courage to move forward, no matter what shadows still lingered in the dark.

13
Return to Paris

Emma gazed out the narrow window of the train, watching the rain streak the glass like tears. The scenery blurred into a grey haze, mirroring the fog inside her mind. Her heart was a jumble of conflicting feelings—relief, fear, hope—each vying for dominance as the miles slipped somewhere between chaos and calm. She had left London with nothing but a battered suitcase and a letter she didn't fully understand, clinging to the hope that Paris might hold answers. The train rattled along, a steady rhythm that contrasted sharply with her pounding thoughts, and somewhere deep inside, she sensed that tonight would mark the beginning of something transformative, whether for better or worse.

Across the car, Liam sat with his head leaned against the window, eyes unfocused. His bag was on the floor, half-unzipped, papers spilling from its confines, as if a part of him was trying to escape from the unspoken weight pressing on him. He'd come to the station seeking quiet inspiration, a last shot at salvage before surrendering to a life of routine and forgetfulness. The storm outside had turned the journey into an ordeal—floods blocking the tracks, delays piling up like bricks on his chest. At first, the delay had been a minor inconvenience, then a nightmare. Yet, as the hours lengthened, an odd sense of anticipation crept over him, a flickering awareness that something meaningful was brewing in this nightly chaos.

Emma caught herself stealing glances at Liam, noting the rough scruff of his beard, the way his fingers tapped nervously on his knee. He looked like someone used to vivid stories, yet tired of fighting the ghosts of memory. And she wondered—was he truly a columnist on a lark, or hiding something darker beneath that tired exterior? Her own secrets simmered just beneath her skin, waiting to surface. In the flickering light of the carriage, shadows cast by the storm danced along the walls, creating windows into their fractured lives—both fragile, both secretly chasing something buried beneath layers of artifice. The air thickened with unspoken truths as the train crept toward Paris, each passenger wrapped in their own tumult, yet bound together by this unplanned captivity.

Then, at Calais, the train came to a shuddering halt with a jarring screech that made Emma clutch her armrest. Outside, the storm struck a fierce toll, the sky weeping in relentless torrents. Outside the window, the platform vanished into shadows, and the distant rumble of thunder threatened to drown out the sounds of hurried footsteps and whispered commands. Emma felt her stomach tighten—what was supposed to be a quick transfer now stretched into hours. She glimpsed Liam grabbing his coat, glancing anxiously at his phone, eyes flickering with suspicion. Their small space suddenly brimmed with a tense energy. Neither spoke, yet the air between them crackled with the knowledge that something unseen was stirring in the darkness beyond the glass, something that was about to change everything.

Back inside, Emma's fingers instinctively reached into her bag, pulling out her sketchpad. She began to draw, the pencil gliding with a practiced ease that betrayed her nerves. Her notes weren't random doodles—they were precise, architectural observations of the train's security features, escape routes, and cameras. Liam caught sight of her hand moving rapidly across the paper, a spark of curiosity lighting his eyes.

"Are you an architect?" he asked softly, leaning closer.

Emma hesitated, then shook her head.

"Just... trying to stay calm."

Her voice was steady, though her trembling fingertips betrayed her. For Liam, it was a subtle sign that she was hiding something, something she wasn't ready—or didn't want—to reveal. The moment hung in the air as the storm raged outside, their secrets cloaked in shadows as the train remained silent, frozen in a night that felt too long, too heavy to bear easily.

Around midnight, the train shuddered again. Liam checked his phone—no signal. His stomach knotted. Then, amidst the darkness, he saw Emma stiffen. She had been watching him, eyes narrowed, lips pressed tight. Without a word, she reached for her bag, withdrawing her phone and a small, well-worn notebook. Liam saw her glance quickly over her shoulder, as if worried about eavesdroppers. When their eyes met, Emma's face was pale, tense. She whispered:

"I saw you talking on your phone earlier. Were you...?"

Liam cut her off gently, voice husky: "Just checking the clock. Nothing more."

But the flicker of suspicion lingered—not because he'd lied, he realized, but because Emma's instincts were sharper than she let on. Outside, the storm's fury grew stronger, and somewhere beyond the rain-soaked glass, an unseen menace moved stealthily in the shadows, waiting for its moment to strike.

Unbeknownst to both, in the depths of that chaos, their lives were slowly entangling. Each passing second drew them closer to truths neither dared to acknowledge. Emma's heart pounded with the same rhythm as the thunder—the same rhythm that told her her grandmother's mysterious letter was not coincidence, and that the storm was merely a curtain concealing what was coming. Liam's mind raced, piecing together fragments of overheard conversations, secretive exchanges, and the strange determination in Emma's guarded silence. In this storm-tossed carriage, wrapped in darkness and danger, they were no longer strangers. They were players in a game far bigger than either of them imagined, walking on the edge of a precipice that would soon pull them into the heart of a darkness they couldn't yet see, but would come to understand too late. The night stretched on, full of shadows and whispers, promising that dawn—and revelation—was just beyond the horizon of fear.

***

The rain had been relentless all night. Water seeped into every crevice, turning the platform into a slick, glistening surface that reflected the dull glow of distant city lights. The train's engine coughed and sputtered, warning signs that it might not move for a while longer. Emma's coat was soaked through, and she clutched her bag tightly, eyes darting around the deserted station. Amidst the chaos of the storm, a lone figure struggled on the far end, dragging a suitcase that seemed to battle against the wind. The man's face was obscured beneath a battered hat and a thick scarf, his posture tense as he looked for a way to get help.

Emma hesitated, then hesitated again. Despite her own troubles—her chest tight with exhaustion and anxiety—she couldn't ignore the man's distress. She took a tentative step forward, her shoes splashing in puddles as she approached. The man looked up, eyes searching beneath the brim of his hat, and when he saw her stepping closer, a faint flicker of relief crossed his face.

"Excuse me," Emma said softly, trying to mask her weariness, "do you need help?"

His voice was rough, edged with exhaustion, but grateful:

"Yes, please," he replied, voice cracking. "I've been stranded for hours, and my phone's dead. I don't know what to do."

He explained that he was a traveler, caught in the same storm that had halted the entire city's transport system. His destination was just a few miles away, but the flooded tracks had grounded everyone. Emma, instinctively empathetic, reached into her bag and pulled out her scarf, wrapping it around his shoulders for warmth.

"There's a cab stand inside the station, but it's probably flooded or closed," she said, trying to sound practical. "I can stay with you a while, see if there's a way to get you out, or at least find someone who can help."

The man nodded gratefully, his hands trembling as he held her sleeve.

"Thank you. I've been wandering these platforms

for hours. It's like the storm has swallowed everything."

As they moved toward the station building, Emma's mind raced. She knew what it felt like—being trapped, uncertain if help was coming, desperate for any sign of safety. Her heart clenched with a strange mixture of compassion and curiosity. Amidst the chaos, she sensed something unusual about the man—something more than just a stranded traveler. His eyes carried a wary alertness, as if he was hiding a secret beneath his tired exterior. Inside the station, the flickering overhead lights cast long shadows over abandoned benches and battered ticket machines. The air smelled of damp paper and old hope, and Emma felt the weight of unseen eyes watching from the dark corners.

He finally settled on a bench near the empty information kiosk, pulling out a crumpled map, trying to figure a way out. Emma looked around, examining the few remaining people—mostly station staff who had managed to seek shelter or were too overwhelmed to notice. Suddenly, she caught sight of a figure in a corner, a shadow moving at the edge of her vision. When she turned, she saw a woman watching them—fingering her handbag, eyes sharp despite her calm exterior. Emma's instincts prickled. Was this woman tied to the trouble somehow? Her gaze lingered as the woman's lips curled into a slight smile, then she turned away, melting into the shadows once more. Emma's pulse quickened, but she said nothing—yet.

The stranger beside her whispered:

"There are some people who don't want us to get out of here. Be cautious."

Emma's breath caught. She wasn't sure if it was the storm, her own rising fear, or the realization that they might be caught in a web far more dangerous than they had imagined. Every corner of the station suddenly felt like a trap waiting to spring. As her mind spun with questions, a distant siren wailed, echoing through the night like a warning. The storm raged on outside, but inside her, a different storm was brewing—one that might threaten to unravel everything she had been trying to protect. Her hand instinctively grasped his sleeve tightly, not just out of kindness, but because she sensed that this night was only just beginning to show its true face.

***

It was as if the train had become a constrained universe, compressed by doubt and the pressing weight of secrets. Emma sat stiffly in her seat, the sketches still clenched in her hand, her eyes flickering between Liam and the darkened window. Every crackle of the overhead speaker felt magnified, each message carried with it a faint echo of danger she could not yet see. The storm's relentless grip had turned their journey into a suspended nightmare, yet beneath that chaos, a new thread was beginning to unravel. Emma's pulse quickened—she sensed it in the air, an unspoken truth waiting to be uncovered, holding her firmly on the edge of discovery.

Liam watched her, noting the slight tremor in her hands, the way her gaze lingered on the empty corridor beyond their compartment. The tension hung between them, thicker than the fog filling the train's murky interior. Somewhere behind his own guarded eyes, a restless curiosity gnawed at him, pushing him deeper into the maze of the mystery. Just hours ago, they'd been only two stranded travelers, each hiding fragments of their past. Now, beneath that veneer, a new clue shimmered—an indication that the shadows shadowing their path ran even deeper. The faint click of Emma's pen against her notebook felt almost like a signal, a subtle whisper urging him to listen more carefully.

Days ago, Emma had brushed aside her own instincts, dismissing the strange sketches she'd slipped into her bag as mere doodles. Now, those drawings seemed to glow with significance. She had captured the train's architecture with an obsessive precision—exits, security cameras, hidden corners—all in a way that suggested knowledge beyond her usual capacity. As she traced the lines with trembling fingers, she recalled a fragment from her grandmother's letter, a time-stamped phrase about "hidden compartments" and "secret passages." Could the sketches be more than mere art practice? Could they be a map, a clue—something that would lead her directly to her grandmother's long-lost treasure, or worse, to the very danger she was trying to escape?

In the silence that followed, Liam leaned forward slightly, his voice low but deliberate.

"You're not just drawing to pass the time, are you?"

His eyes held a mixture of suspicion and curiosity.

Emma hesitated, then shook her head slowly, her lips pressed in a thin line.

"It's not just sketches. It's... something I saw, something I remember from my grand-mother's stories."

Her voice barely rose above a whisper. Liam's brow furrowed, and as he reached out subtly, his fingers grazed her notebook, sensing its importance. Outside, lightning flashed, illuminating the storm like a jagged scar across the sky, hinting at chaos beyond the train's walls. The storm wasn't just delaying their journey; it was a barrier, a gate that kept something dangerous just out of reach—something that might now be slipping into their realm.

Later that night, in the flickering candlelight of the compartment, Emma's mind replayed the moment she overheard Liam's urgent conversation. As the train stopped in Amiens, her ears caught snippets of his hurried speech—words spoken in a language she didn't understand completely. She had been peeking through the crack of the door when she heard him mention "the package," "tomorrow," and "priority." The cryptic exchange sent a jolt through her spine, her heart pounding in sync with the thunder outside. She had thought Liam was just a wandering writer, a man lost in his own troubles, but now she saw the cracks in his calm exterior. Was he involved in something more entangled? Was he hiding a secret that linked directly back to her grandmother's mysterious past? Trust was slipping away, thread by thread, as the danger grew more tangible.

Emma curled her fingers into fists, feeling the cold metal of her ring, a reminder of how tangled her life had become—work, love, secrets all collapsing into one another. Her mind refused to let go of the letter, the cryptic words about "treasure," "resistance," and "truth." This wasn't coincidence. Somehow, her grandmother's past had cast a shadow long enough to reach into her present, infecting every page of her life. The revelation that someone on this train might be watching, waiting, to strike at just the right moment, made her breath shallow. She wondered if Liam sensed it too. If he'd noticed the way her jaw tightened when a new shadow crossed her path or the way her eyes darted to every stranger in the carriage who might be more than they appeared to be.

As the night deepened, the atmosphere shifted from uneasy silence to a gathering storm of questions and possibilities. Emma knew she had to act. Every clue, every sketch, every whispered word in the dark was a piece of a larger puzzle. Her grandmother's words echoed: "Find the truth within the shadows—they hide the key." Her fingers trembled as she looked once more at her sketches—images not just of a train, but of secret doors, hidden chambers, and safe passages. Something was hidden beneath the veneer of her ordinary life, and it was waiting for her to find it. She caught Liam staring at her again, and for a fleeting second, she saw a flicker of acknowledgment—a silent promise that, somehow, they would face whatever was coming together. Because now, more than ever, their lives depended on it.

14
The Next Adventure Begins

The room beneath Montmartre's winding streets was silent, save for the faint echo of footsteps above. Emma's fingers trembled as she traced the outline of the small, concealed door she'd discovered behind a false wall in the hidden chamber. The air was thick with dust and the scent of aged parchment, memories buried for decades. Every corner of this secret space hinted at stories long forgotten, but Emma's heart pounded with the realization that she was closer than ever to uncovering her grandmother's true legacy. She pressed her palm against the cool, carved stone, feeling the faint buzz of anticipation ripple through her veins.

Liam lingered at the threshold, his eyes scanning the shadowed passageways that led deeper into the labyrinth. Shadows danced as his flashlight flickered, illuminating a jumble of crates, maps, and journals stacked haphazardly against the walls. His mind raced, piecing together the fragments of what they'd uncovered—records of stolen art, coded messages, and references to a clandestine network stretching across Europe. This wasn't just about some long-lost treasure; it was a history smuggled and concealed, secrets so old they seemed almost sacred. The weight of their discovery pressed upon them, intertwining the threads of their own lives with those buried relics of the past.

Emma's eyes welled with tears as she uncovered a leather-bound journal, its pages brittle from age. Flipping through, she found meticulous notes in her grandmother's handwriting—sketches of paintings, lists of suspicious transactions, markings that corresponded to places along the train routes they'd been following. Suddenly, a photograph slipped from between the pages, catching the dim light—a faded image of a young woman, arms linked with a man in a Resistance uniform, standing proudly beside a hidden door just like the one now before Emma. Her breath hitched. This was the evidence that would shake everything they thought they knew about her family. Her grandmother's secret empire wasn't just a tale of art theft, it was a web that spanned generations, unbreakable and dark.

The distant sound of footsteps above made Liam's blood run cold. Someone was coming. Emma's hand instinctively reached for the journal, clutching it tightly. Liam signaled silently, his eyes narrowing as he studied the corridor's narrowing silhouette. They both knew they weren't alone—their presence in these forbidden tunnels was a threat to those who had meticulously guarded their secrets all these years. Every creak of the old stone, every whisper of the wind through concealed passages, heightened their alertness. The quiet morphed into a tense silence, broken only by the pounding of their own hearts. Whatever secret lay beyond that small wooden door, it was now within reach—and trouble was tracking them, closing in fast.

Emma hesitated, then pushed open the door with a soft click. Inside, a small room revealed itself, filled with stacks of faded artifacts, rolled canvases, and boxes marked with cryptic symbols. She moved slowly, her fingers tracing the carvings: a series of intertwined circles, a symbol she recognized from her grandmother's notes. The walls were lined with further documents—photographs of stolen masterpieces, ledger entries, and handwritten codes. Liam entered behind her, the weight of the discovery pressing on his shoulders. This wasn't just about hidden art; it was about a long history of betrayal, deception, and lies buried beneath the very streets of Montmartre. Emma's pulse fluttered—she was standing at the crossroads of truth and myth, with everything she thought she knew threatening to crumble beneath her feet.

Suddenly, a faint beep cut through the silence—an alert from Emma's phone. She froze, realizing that her device was still active, still transmitting. Panic flickered across her face as she looked at Liam. Had they been compromised all along? Her fingers rapidly brushed the screen, trying to disconnect, but the device's screen flickered ominously. A message appeared:

"Remove the device, or they'll find you."

Emma's stomach clenched. Someone was watching. Someone knew they were here. The lives they had been chasing, the secrets they were uncovering—all tied to a deadly game. And now, the stakes had escalated beyond their control. Shadows moved at the edge of the room as the realization dawned: their every step was being watched, and the hidden past that was meant to stay buried was about to rewrite their future forever.

***

The air in the Montmartre apartment was thick with anticipation, each breath heavy with secrets long buried. Emma's fingertips trembled as she traced the faded edges of the photographs and documents she had uncovered. The walls around her seemed to pulse with ghostly memories, whispering of a past she dared not fully confront. Every step she took echoed with the weight of history—her grandmother's hidden life, the lies woven into her family's legacy. The silence was deafening, broken only by the faint rustle of papers and the distant hum of the city below, calling her to move forward but anchoring her with the ghosts she tried to forget.

Outside, the late evening shadows stretched across the cobblestones, cloaking the streets in a blanket of dusk. Liam stood near the narrow window, eyes fixed on the bustling alley beneath. The truth they'd uncovered in the secret chambers beneath the apartment was staggering—records of stolen art, transactions seamless as threads in a spider's web, all spun over decades. Every document was a piece of a puzzle she had once thought shattered forever. Emma's revelations about her grandmother's true role sent a shiver through him—here they were, in the heart of Paris, face to face with a legacy that threatened to crush them. The air crackled with the electric charge of impending confrontation, and he knew the moment was near when all their plans and hopes would be tested.

As Emma carefully packed the fragile evidence into a battered leather satchel, her mind raced through the possibilities. Margot's betrayal, the web of lies, and the dark secrets that had sustained her criminal empire for decades—all these pieces now converged in her hands. The sacrifice of her family, the stolen images, the forged records—all of it led here, to this moment of reckoning. She clenched her fists, feeling the sting of adrenaline sharpen her senses. They had come so far, driven by the ghosts of the past and a desperate need to set things right. Yet, beneath her resolve, a flicker of doubt lingered—could they expose everything without paying a terrible price? The clock seemed to grind to a halt, the only sound the distant clatter of a train reminding her of the journey still unfinished, waiting to be completed. The climax loomed, just beyond the horizon of her fears, promising either justice or disaster.

***

The morning sun barely pierced the cloud cover as Emma stood by the window of the cramped train carriage, clutching her bag tightly. Outside, the landscape blurred past in shades of gray: fields soaked from last night's rain, leafless trees scrambling for the sky, and distant silhouettes of villages slipping into the mist. Every mile they left behind felt like shedding a layer of her old life, but beneath her calm exterior, a storm of nerves churned. Her heart beat a little faster each time the train jolted over uneven tracks, shadows of doubt intertwining with hope. The air in the carriage was thick with unspoken tension, the quiet punctuated only by the rhythmic clatter of wheels on rails and her own racing thoughts.

Beside her, Liam shifted in his seat, eyes fixed on the horizon even as he tried to focus on the passing scenery. His brow was furrowed, not just from the bumpy ride but from the weight of secrets both shared and hidden. The storm outside had caught them unprepared, turning what should have been a simple journey into a test of patience—and endurance. The late hour meant most passengers had settled into uneasy silence, some staring out windows, others lost in their own worlds. Emma caught Liam glancing at her occasionally, a flicker of something she couldn't quite place—curiosity, suspicion, or maybe just the exhaustion crowding into his eyes. Whatever it was, their shared predicament was about to push them toward a decision neither fully understood yet.

As the storm rumbled closer, muffling the distant thunder, Emma's fingers traced the edges of her grandmother's mysterious letter. The note had been tucked inside a crumbling photo album, brittle and yellowing with age, but the words were clear: a "treasure" hidden in Montmartre, awaiting discovery. That letter was her only clue—her last connection to a woman she never truly knew, yet whose shadow haunted her every step. She thought about her grandmother's resistance days, the secrets she'd kept for decades, and now—here, on this floating metal cage—those secrets seemed to pulse with life, demanding answers. Emma's pulse quickened; something told her this journey wouldn't just be about reaching Paris but about uncovering truths buried deep beneath layers of history and deception.

Across from her, Liam finally broke the silence, voice low but with a hint of excitement hiding beneath weariness.

"You know, I've seen a lot of unexpected stops in my travels," he said, glancing at her with a half-smile. "But this storm turning our trip into a kind of temporary exile—it's a story in itself."

Emma nodded, offering a faint smile, yet her mind was a thousand miles away.

The flickering of the train's emergency lights cast shifting shadows on their faces, momentarily transforming strangers into conspirators, allies in this unfolding mystery. Liam's eyes flicked to her sketchbook, sensing the subtle determination in her posture. In that quiet, unspoken exchange, an understanding formed—whatever lay ahead, they would face it together, stepping into the unknown with only a shared resolve and hopes for answers that might forever change their lives.

And then, in the dim glow of the cabin, Emma saw Liam's face shift. His gaze flickered to a small, discreet device in his hand—the one he'd brought secretly into the carriage. He murmured something into it, voice subdued, words foreign and clipped. A quick, almost imperceptible nod, and then silence. Emma's stomach clenched. Her instincts prickled; something was off. The way he'd paused, the urgency in his voice—what was he hiding? A fleeting thought crossed her mind: maybe he was just nervous, or maybe he had a reason to keep secrets, but in that moment, the thread of her uncertainty tightened. Her muscles tensed as she remembered her grandmother's warnings—warnings about trusting too easily, about dangers lurking beneath familiar faces. The train's rhythmic rumble seemed thunderous now, echoing the pounding of her own heart, as she wondered if the horizon they were rushing toward was hiding truths far darker than storms or waiting shadows.

Further down the corridor, the faint hum of voices

drifted from a neighboring carriage—another delay, another story unfolding in whispers. Emma closed her eyes for a moment, trying to steady her breath. Outside, rain started to lash against the windows, each drop a drumbeat of impending revelation. Somewhere in that storm, her destination loomed—a place her grandmother swore held answers, but also danger. Emma's fingers tightened around the letter, the paper felt like a talisman against the uncertainty. A gust of wind rattled the carriage door, and for a second, she thought she saw a shadow slipping past in the darkness, silent and purposeful. Her mind raced with images of Montmartre—the winding alleys, secret rooms, hidden passages—places her grandmother might have concealed secrets. How many lies or truths were buried in those old sketches and soaked-in stories? The night was stretching long, and with each passing mile, Emma felt the weight of history crashing toward her, ready to rewrite her own story along the way. The horizon whispered promises of answers, but as the storm threatened to swallow the sky, she knew that the real revelation was only just beginning."

15
Epilogue: Love and Legacy

Emma settled into the soft murmur of her small apartment in Montmartre, the city's muted hum wrapping around her like an old familiar coat. It was strange, how peaceful she felt now, after months of chaos and shadows. The faint scent of fresh baguette and the distant chime of church bells became a lullaby she never knew she needed. Yet beneath that calm, a quiet tension simmered, echoing the secrets she'd uncovered and the storm that still lurked beyond her door.

London seemed worlds away, yet her mind sometimes wandered there, tracing the outline of her old life with a bittersweet ache. The empty gallery spaces, the face of her ex-fiancé frozen in her memory, and the weight of her unspoken truths. She had traded heartbreak for quiet discovery, steering her days with understated purpose. Often, she would walk through the narrow streets of Montmartre, her footsteps light yet deliberate, as if searching for a hidden door or a missing piece in her family's puzzle. No one knew the truth she carried, not even Liam, who now shared her silent life, a constant presence in her days.

Across the Channel, Liam's life had settled into a different rhythm. His mornings began with a slow cup of coffee, the kind that felt like an act of rebellion against the rush he used to chase in war zones. His writing desk faced a window overlooking a quiet London street, a place where he could breathe without the distant roar of explosions. The interruptions of his past—the panic attacks, the ghosts of memories he couldn't shake—still haunted him, but here, in the subdued light, he found moments of peace. Yet beneath that surface, a restless part of him wondered if his remaining days could be filled with stories worth telling, stories more about hope than despair.

Her routine was interrupted one evening when a letter arrived—a faded, rubber-stamped envelope bearing her grandmother's handwriting. Emma's hands trembled as she opened it, revealing a crumbling sheet of paper filled with hurried script and a final, cryptic message: a name, a date, and a simple instruction to look beneath the oldest stone in Montmartre. It was the first inkling that her quiet life was just a fragile veneer over something far more dangerous. Liam, reading over her shoulder, felt a flicker of recognition and unease. Something about the letter prickled at the back of his mind, whispering that their peaceful days might be numbered, and that beneath this calm surface, storms waited patiently, ready to break free.

***

The room was dimly lit, shadows flickering along the cracked plaster walls as Emma cautiously stepped forward. The air was thick with dust and the faint scent of old canvas and forgotten secrets. She brushed her fingers over a crumbling bookcase, its shelves sagging under the weight of years, each one hiding whispers of a past she was only beginning to understand. The secret apartment beneath Montmartre had been more than a hideout; it was a vault of history, scars from a war that refused to fade. Emma's heart hammered in her chest, her fingertips tingling as she traced the outline of a hidden lever concealed behind a row of faded paintings. Just beyond, the faint click echoed softly in the silence, a signal that she had found what she'd been hunting for—if only she could decipher its message.

Liam followed closely behind, his eyes darting around the cluttered space as if expecting the shadows themselves to spring to life. His breath was shallow; every breath was a gamble, as if the very walls were watching, waiting to reveal what had been kept secret for decades. The whispers of history seemed to murmur from every corner—indistinct voices from the past, urging him to listen. The photographs, torn documents, and rusted artifacts all hinted at a story buried deep beneath the surface of Montmartre. They had come too far to turn back now, but the stakes had ratcheted higher with each passing second. Somewhere in this maze of secrecy lay the truth, and Emma knew—more than ever—that her grandmother's hidden legacy was connected to all of it, tangled in the shadows of this clandestine labyrinth.

With trembling hands, Emma pulled the lever, revealing a hidden passage that spiraled downward, washed in a faint, orange glow from an underground lantern. The air grew colder, heavier, as if the tunnel had been waiting patiently for this moment. Liam drew his phone, flicking on the flashlight, its beam piercing through the darkness, illuminating a narrow corridor lined with worn stones and old brickwork. Their footsteps echoed softly against the cold walls, each step bringing them closer to a truth that could rewrite history. Emma's mind raced—what secrets did her grandmother hide that necessitated such cunning? And what lay at the end of this passage—a treasure, a trap, or something far worse?

As they pressed onward, muffled sounds emerged from ahead—whispered voices hinting at clandestine meetings or perhaps the echoes of a past conspiracy. Emma's pulse quickened; the weight of her revelation pressed down on her like a stone. She glanced at Liam, whose steady gaze betrayed no fear, only determination. In that moment, the two understood that they had become part of a story far larger than themselves, one stitched into the very fabric of Montmartre's hidden corridors. Somewhere there, in the shadows and secrets, lay the evidence they sought—a trove of records and artifacts that could shatter decades of lies. But as they drew closer, a chilling thought seized them: they were not alone. Someone was waiting for them, lurking in the darkness, ready to defend their secrets at any cost.

Their flashlights suddenly flickered, plunging the tunnel into darkness. The air grew tense, charged with a strange static that made their hair stand on end. Emma froze, listening—there was a faint scuffing, a whisper of movement. Liam's voice broke the silence, quiet but urgent:

"Stay close."

Just then, a figure emerged from the shadows—clad in dark clothes, eyes gleaming with an unsettling calm. Emma's breath hitched as recognition flashed through her—this was no ordinary trespasser. It was someone who knew every inch of this labyrinth, someone who had been waiting for them. The figure raised a hand slowly, revealing a small, ornate box—a sign that whatever was inside was worth risking everything to protect. Emma's mind raced, heart pounding. She knew, in that instant, their discovery had true enemies—and they were prepared to fight for every secret buried here.

***

In the quiet dawn that seeped through the curtains of their modest Paris apartment, Emma found herself sitting by the window, a steaming cup of coffee warming her hands. The city around her was waking up, its streets already humming with life, yet inside, her mind was a storm of memories and promises. She reflected on how love had slipped into her life quietly, with Liam's steady presence replacing the chaos that once overshadowed her. Their journey together had begun amidst danger and deception, but now, in these gentle hours, it transformed into something more fragile and precious—a foundation for hope.

Liam entered the room softly, carrying a folder of photographs and notes from their previous night's strategizing. His eyes lingered on Emma's face, tracing the soft lines of exhaustion mixed with determination. They had uncovered so much — secrets that had threatened to rip their worlds apart — yet here they were, still standing, still fighting. Love, they realized, wasn't just about passion or fleeting moments; it was a bond forged in shared peril, in whispered fears and silent trust. He reached out without a word, gently brushing a lock of hair from her face, offering silent reassurance that together, they could carve out a new beginning from the remnants of their pasts.

Their pasts—so tangled and full of shadows—had been the reason they met, yet now, they saw them as stepping stones rather than barriers. Emma's grandmother's story, once a distant mystery, had suddenly colored their entire world with shades of truth and deception. Emma's fingertips traced the edges of her grandmother's old journal, now filled with coded entries and photographs of stolen artworks. It was more than a legacy of theft; it was a testament to survival, resilience, and the complex threads that tie families together—even when buried beneath layers of crime and betrayal. With each revelation, they felt the weight of history pressing upon their shoulders, whispering both warnings and promises of redemption.

They moved carefully through the apartment, their movements deliberate as if treading over fragile glass.

Emma knew the final pieces of the puzzle were close—she could feel it in her bones. The truth about Margot's treachery had been buried deep, hidden behind decades of silence, yet the evidence was within reach. Liam, as always, saw the bigger picture. His undercover work had revealed cracks in law enforcement's façade, shadows of corruption lurking beneath a veneer of integrity. They both understood that the stakes had never been higher. The name Margot Dubois had become a symbol of the past's haunting grip, but now, it was poised to be erased—or redeemed.

Their plan was simple on paper—reach the hidden rooms beneath Montmartre, uncover the records, and expose the network—but the reality was far more dangerous. Emma's hand trembled as she recalled the countless clues she'd pieced together, and how each one pointed to her grandmother's true nature. Margot's story was one of manipulation, a woman who had used her war-time alliances to hide her darker deeds. Emma's purpose now was clear: unearth the truth, face the shadows, and shine a light on the lies. Liam's role was equally vital—his camera and microphone could broadcast their findings to the world, but only if they managed to survive the dangers lurking around every corner of that labyrinth beneath Montmartre.

As they descended into the secret tunnels, a cold chill ran through the air. The passageways twisted like a serpent, hidden shelves lined with artifacts, documents, and remnants of a long-forgotten empire. Emma's heart hammered as she studied the faint markings on the walls, realizing these passages had been used for more than storage—they were strategic lairs crafted by those desperate to escape justice. Every step brought them closer to revelations that could shatter their lives forever. Shadows danced unpredictably in the flickering light, and a distant, muffled sound made Emma stop abruptly. Was it footsteps—or something more sinister? The dread that had been lurking at the edges of her mind suddenly sharpened into focus, a nerve that prickled with the sense that the final battle was imminent.

Then, the faint hum of voices echoed through the silence. Emma and Liam pressed themselves against the cold stone, exchanging tense glances. They were no longer alone in the dark. Armed with little more than their instincts, they prepared for what was to come—the moment to confront the deepest lies, the people who had been deceiving them all along. Every secret record, every hiding place, seemed to pulse with unseen energy, as if the very walls were waiting for their moment to reveal its truth. As Emma clutched her grandmother's journal tighter, she knew the final revelation was near. Somewhere in this labyrinth, the answers they had fought for all along waited to be uncovered, even if it meant facing the darkness that threatened to swallow them whole.